LISSA, BEAUTIFUL

A FUTURISTIC ROMANCE RETELLING OF THE FROG PRINCESS

A.W. CROSS

Lissa, Beautiful

Copyright © 2019 by Glory Box Press

Published by Glory Box Press
British Columbia, Canada.
gloryboxpress@gmail.com

All rights reserved. This book or any portion thereof may not be reproduced or used in any manner whatsoever without the express written permission of the publisher except for the use of brief quotations in a book review. For information regarding permission, write to Glory Box Press at gloryboxpress@gmail.com

First edition, 2020

ISBN 978-1-9995711-9-1

Cover design by Danielle Fine
Interior design and formatting by Glory Box Press
Editing by Danielle Fine

This is a work of fiction. Names, characters, businesses, places, events, and incidents are either the products of the author's imagination or used in a fictitious manner. Any resemblance to actual persons, living or dead, or actual events is purely coincidental.

FOR H, AND THE
WILDWOOD WITHIN.

LISSA, BEAUTIFUL

ONE

The sun hung hot and heavy in the cloudless sky. Good. Lissa still had time before the things that slept in the day uncurled from their hiding places to stalk the Wildwood, bathed in moonlight and wreathed in the smoke forever seeping through the Perimeter.

The smoke always made Lissa's throat itch, but it had gotten even worse since they'd started using that damned Foxwept Tar. Idiots. The Wildwood was already adapting, and it wouldn't be long before even the incendiary gel couldn't hold it back. Then what would they do?

She didn't need to go any closer to the edge to know what she would see. For years, a seemingly eternal battle had raged between the encroaching Wildwood and Foxwept Province's military, red and black fatigues marking human and android soldiers alike.

Speaking of which.

The hair on the back of Lissa's neck rose, prickling under her collar. There was something watching her, something not of the Wood.

She skirted the edge of the Perimeter, careful to keep out of sight. It wasn't illegal to live in the Wildwood, but it was still better not to be seen. There was always the odd soldier with a hero complex who didn't understand why anyone would *choose* to reside in the distorted wilderness. Even those living close to the flaming Perimeter had to endure a certain amount of suspicion.

Still, the soldiers were better than the rest of Foxwept Province, who viewed the people of the Wood as degenerate bumpkins—backwood and backward, clinging to trees and hiding in the shadows from the danger that constantly stalked them.

Lissa snorted. Living in the Wildwood was safe enough if you respected it and kept your wits about you. The problem was, not everyone did—tourists with romantic views of the dangerous wilderness were the worst—and it brought unwelcome attention to the rest of them. It had been nearly eight years since the disaster that had created the monstrous wilds, and every year brought more thrill-seekers in search of bragging rights for braving the terrible Wildwood.

Until they ended up being bitten, stung, poisoned, or one of a hundred other things. And then, of course, someone had to rescue them, and the Wildwood once again came under scrutiny, and its inhabitants—the ones too stubborn, too poor, or too hunted by the law—held their breaths, waiting to see if this would be the time the governor of Foxwept Province finally sat up and paid attention. Invariably, the storm would pass, and the province's attention would refocus on solvable problems.

Ugh. Best to just find the plant and get back. Swift could get his own accursed sap next time. He knew how much she detested getting this close to the world outside the Wildwood, and still, every time he needed something near the border, he would ask her to get it, even though he was more than capable of doing it himself. So why did she keep agreeing?

Because I'm pathetic, that's why.

The closer she was to the Perimeter, the closer she was to the rest of Foxwept Province, and its capital city, Portfade. To *life*. To a world she desperately wanted to belong to, but never would.

All because of her…difference. Swift thought she should march around all of Foxwept with her head held high, but for Lissa, accepting that she had to live with something and being *proud* of it was not the same thing. Besides, it was all right for him to say that—he at least *looked* normal.

And it wasn't like she hadn't tried. When she was younger, she'd gone to Portfade on errands with her mother, had even enrolled in school there. On the first day of classes she'd been so full of foolish hope, buoyed by the diversity of faces around her. She'd known it wouldn't be easy, but…

But the taunts, the cruel nicknames still haunted her. Even the teacher hadn't been able to meet her eyes. All because they could see what she was. How would they react if they knew there were others like her, people whose oddness couldn't readily be seen? Would it matter? Or would those folks be accepted because they had the civility to keep their true selves hidden?

In her case, it made no difference either way. Hiding what she was would draw nearly as much suspicion and attention, so in the end, she kept to the Wildwood. There, surrounded by strangeness, she could almost ignore the shame that burned under her abominable skin.

Almost. In her weaker moments, she resented herself more than those who'd teased her. She could've been stronger, could've refused to let her fear and embarrassment hold her prisoner. But she had, and if she was honest with herself, she still did.

A musky, honeyed scent on the air broke her reverie. *There.* The plant she'd been searching for. She winced. It seemed even bigger than normal and again she cursed Swift under her breath.

Let's get this over with. She dropped her backpack to the ground and rooted through it, before pulling out a pair of long mesh gloves. She slid them over her hands then tugged them as far past her elbows as they would go. Hopefully, it would be protection enough.

Ignoring the sweat trickling down between her shoulder blades, Lissa approached the large plant, trying to disturb the air as little as possible. The corpselure was nearly as tall as she was, its mouth wider than her arm-span. At the moment, its barbed maw was closed, the long spikes interlocked in an impenetrable barrier, guarding the prize within. It swayed on its thick stalk as she stepped closer, and she closed her eyes and took a steadying breath.

Slow. Nice and slow.

Millions of fine golden hairs sprouted from the fleshy green stalk, giving the plant an almost cuddly appearance, but Lissa wasn't fooled. She'd seen the jaws of a corpselure clamp down on the neck of a curious deer more than once, suspending it mercilessly above the ground until the corrosive sap liberated its head from its body.

Only the quickest to learn survived in the Wildwood.

Which is another reason Swift sent you instead of coming himself; he knows better than to go around tickling carnivorous plants. Some best friend.

But she'd promised. And it wasn't like she was doing it for free. The tiny automaton bird Swift had promised to build for her in exchange was well worth the risk.

Except that he'd probably have made it for you anyway.

The plant shifted again, its jaws parting slightly as though it were tasting the air.

It suspects I'm here. I've got to do it now, before it's certain.

Tugging up her gloves once more, she grabbed the special vial and approached the corpselure, stretching out her hand while leaning as far back as she could. She ran the vial lightly over the golden hairs, and the great mouth snapped open, the crimson flesh inside as hypnotic as a beating heart. Pooled in the bottom jaw was the glistening, deadly sap she'd come to collect.

If it didn't bite her arm off first. How long would Swift wait before coming to find her? Hours? Days? *Weeks?*

She shook her head. *Stop being ridiculous. Just do it before you lose your nerve.*

Smoothly, she dipped the vial into the viscous liquid, careful not to touch the barbed lips. There, just a bit more and—

A blur of movement in the corner of her eye was the only warning before something hard struck her on the back of her head. Her arm jerked involuntarily and, in terrifying slow motion, the steel trap of the jaws began to snap shut. She wrenched her hand back as quickly as she could, and she was almost free, almost safe, when one of the barbs caught her, just above the cuff of her glove. Fire burned a trail up her arm to her shoulder as venom bit into her flesh, the pain so sudden and overwhelming that she stood there with her mouth agape, staring at the red spokes snaking up her arm, scorching their image into her retinas so deeply she could still see them long after the dark of unconsciousness swallowed her whole.

TWO

Will he never shut up?

In his mind's eye, Artem stood, walked with his plate to the head of the table where his father droned on and on, lifted the heavy pewter dish high, and brought it crashing down on the old man's head. Maybe then, with gravy and blood dripping down his face, he would finally stop talking.

Or at least talk about something different. Lately, it seemed all his father wanted to discuss was his children's obligations to the business, to the family.

To *him*.

And no matter how Artem looked at it, it was bad news. When he was younger, he, the second—and as such, lesser—son, had been naïve enough to think he might one day be able to have a life beyond this family, away from his father's shadow and the shade of his dealings. He would see the world, would live where no one knew who he was, where they didn't duck their heads and cross to the other side of the street when they saw him coming.

He'd been such a fool. The best he could truly hope for was to become another faceless, nameless member of the firm. At least then he might get an occasional break from his father's relentless scrutiny.

"Which brings me to my next announcement."

Andrei looked at each of his three children in turn. "Luka will no longer inherit my title as head of Paragon. Instead, the three of you will compete for it." The corner of his mouth quirked in anticipation.

Luka took the bait first, roaring his disbelief. Artem closed his eyes.

His father must be loving this, dangling the bloody carcass of their future over his children's heads like they were a pack of wolves. *He's hoping we'll tear each other apart.* And he would probably get his wish.

Paragon was the umbrella that covered the Volkovs' true business dealings in a layer of respectability so translucent Artem marveled at the endurance of the whole charade. No one with a brain in their heads could believe there was anything decent about them—including Artem.

His whole life he'd endured the stares, the whispers, the distance that separated him from the rest of Foxwept. It was as though he wore a mark, a burning brand that warned others to stay away or risk their lives. If only they knew how powerless he really was. For years, he'd tried to extricate himself from Paragon and his father's hold, so slowly and subtly that by the time the old man realized, it would be too late.

Luka will no longer inherit my title. Artem's time had run out.

Luka had always believed he would automatically become head of the family, and so had his siblings. Ever since they were born, Artem and Misha had watched from the sidelines as Luka was groomed for inescapable success. And now? If Luka was having the title snatched away from him, something was going on. Something big.

The sharp crack of Luka's fist smashing onto the table in front of him snapped Artem's attention back to the present. He straightened in his chair, the skin on the back of his neck prickling as though his father's jaws had already closed around it. Luka's chest heaved, his gaze darting wildly around the room as though he couldn't decide who to blame. It landed on Artem for only a split second before turning toward the *real* threat.

Misha.

In contrast to Luka's anger and Artem's silence, their father's announcement was greeted with pleasure by his third child. She narrowed her eyes and grinned, a smile dripping with corrosive malice. Had she suspected what their father was up to? Either way, Luka was in trouble. Artem had no interest in taking the title—just the opposite. But Misha…she'd often chafed at the restrictions placed on her by their father because of her sex. But now, in only moments, the playing field had become level.

Luka was just getting started. "But *why*? Why would you suddenly— I mean, how could you choose one of *them*—" He brushed off his siblings like flecks of dirt on his suit jacket. "Over me? I've spent my entire life doing everything you—"

"Told you to do. Yes, Luka, I'm aware. And that's part of the problem." He gave his eldest son an ironic grin. "You don't know how to *think*." He rapped on his temple with his knuckles. "Anyway, the title can still be yours. You just have to *earn* it now."

Earn it. A place in their own family, if it could even be called that. Their father had raised them to be wary of each other, to know that although loyalty to the *family* meant everything, blood itself meant *nothing*. So the siblings had circled each other all their lives, watching and waiting.

For an opportunity just like this. The dogfight they'd trained for their whole lives. Well, Artem wanted nothing to do with it.

"Shut up, Luka." His father's voice was soft but carried all the force of an apocalypse.

Luka shut up.

"Whoever ends up leading this family has to be smart. Ruthless. Resourceful. Therefore, we're going to have a little contest. And whoever wins will inherit everything."

"So what's your plan?" Luka recovered quickly, his expression now one of fierce determination. Life had long since taught him there was no point arguing with their father, who couldn't have cared less that Luka had already devoted his life to being his understudy. No, the only way to reclaim his position was to *win*. And Luka knew it.

"We're going to propose a ridiculously lowball sum to purchase the Wildwood from the province."

Buy the *Wildwood*? An out-of-control, predatory, mutated jungle? *And do what with it, exactly?* He'd have thought Father would want to avoid any connection to the mutant forest—he may not have caused the blight with his own hands, but his funding had certainly made it possible.

Luka echoed Artem's thoughts. "Are you mad? Whatever the devil for?" He shook his head but couldn't stop the hope that crept into his eyes. "This must be a joke."

Father crossed his arms over his chest. "It's no joke. And I expect you to show more respect in the future."

Still Luka persevered. "But what do you plan to do with it? This could sink our whole—"

Father held up his hand and again, well-trained, Luka snapped his mouth shut. "There've been some rumors of certain resources in the Wildwood, resources which, if discovered and exploited on land we own, could make us richer than our wildest dreams." He paused dramatically, undoubtedly to see the effect this had on his errant offspring.

Richer than his family's dreams? That was unreasonably rich. *This is going to be a bloodbath.*

Misha's eyes glittered, the gaze of a predator whose prey was completely oblivious to its presence. Artem shuddered. Hopefully she would never look at him like that. "What kind of resources?"

Father smirked. "Medications, exotic plants, and animals…narcotics." He lifted his chin, as though expecting his children to protest.

"Isn't the Wildwood dangerous?" Misha tapped her gold fingernails against her teeth, and Artem itched to hold her down and file them off.

But she *was* right. The Wildwood was incredibly dangerous; everybody knew that. Years ago, scientists in the Blackmoth Republic—backed by 'businessmen' like his father—had genetically engineered crops to increase yields in the agricultural land in the west of the country, thinking that the success would ensure bountiful harvests and keep the entire Republic fed, plus put it on the map for exports. Oh, and make its investors an obscene amount of money.

The results had been monstrous. Literally. Plants and animals mutated and grew out of control, spreading across the landscape like a plague, impervious to pesticides and herbicides. The tangle had spread so far and so quickly that it had nearly pushed the habitants of Foxwept Province into the ocean. Now, nearly eight years later, the military could barely keep it contained as it rapidly adapted to anything they could throw at it. The newest invention, an incendiary gel called Foxwept Tar, was currently the only thing holding it back. And for how much longer?

And this—this jungle of killer plants and ferocious mutant beasts—was what Father believed would be the key to his kingdom? The day just got weirder and weirder.

"Yes, it is. Very dangerous. But that works to our advantage. Nobody else wants to touch that land, and the government would be happy to have the inconvenience and expense of it off their hands for a pittance. Then once it's mi—ours..." His father looked way too pleased with himself, like nothing could possibly go wrong with his insane plan. Had all the power finally rotted his brain?

Well, we all know what pride comes before. Artem snorted to himself. As if he'd ever be that lucky. "So where do we come in?" Artem asked. *And how can I get as far away from it as possible?*

"You three will be responsible for reconnaissance."

"Meaning?"

"You'll go into the Wildwood and find its secrets. Whichever of you brings back the most valuable information will inherit."

If we come back at all. Was that also part of his father's plan? Artem didn't intend to find out. He wasn't going to risk his life for something he didn't even want. Let Luka and Misha fight to the death over it. He would stay where he'd always been—in the shadows, out of the way. In fact...

His heart picked up its rhythm and he fought to

keep his expression neutral. This could be the chance he'd been waiting for. Let Luka and Misha go for each other's throats. In the meantime, while his father's eyes were on them, Artem could make his escape. He'd been squirreling money away for years in the hope that one day he would be able to get beyond his father's clutches and see the rest of the world, like a normal person. He added up the figures in his head. He had enough for a couple of years, if he lived frugally. After that, well, he would just have to see. At least he would be away from here. From *him*.

Artem threw his napkin over the remains of his breakfast and stretched before pushing himself away from the table. His mind raced. What should he do first? What should he pack? He would wait until his brother and sister were safely tucked away on their mission, then he would—

Father's voice brought him up short. "Where do you think you're going?"

He shrugged, fighting to push down his excitement and keep his tone casual. Freedom was close, so close... "To get started. The sooner the better, right?"

"I haven't finished."

It seemed he would have to play his father's game a little longer.

Don't make him suspicious.

Artem lowered himself slowly back into his seat. Luka stared daggers at him, the corner of his mouth twitching. Maybe he shouldn't have pretended to be so eager. The last thing he needed was Luka focusing on him.

If only I could tell him I don't want anything to do with it.

But would he even believe Artem if he did? Not likely in this family.

His father continued. "Whoever returns with the most valuable information, the best way to exploit the Wildwood and turn a fortune off it, gets *everything*."

Misha's heavily shadowed eyes widened. She obviously hadn't accounted for *that*. It would've been funny if it wasn't likely to make her even more dangerous. "Everything? Do you mean—"

"Yes. Everything. And the other two will get *nothing*. You'll be cut off. No place in the company, no money, no trust fund, no inheritance. *Nothing*."

Artem's sister stuck out her lower lip, like she did every time she didn't get her own way. It was incongruous with the rage in her eyes. "But you can't do that! It's not—"

"Fair? No, it's not. But it's not fair that you all get everything handed to you either. You know bloody well I—"

At this point, Artem tuned out. He'd heard this story a million times before. How his father was a self-made man. How his family had been poor, and he'd had to pull himself out of the mud with nobody to help him. Well, except for the wealthy young woman he'd married, who'd conveniently died after giving him three children and taken the secret of his fortune's origins with her to her grave.

Father couldn't mean it, though, could he? He was a bastard, but even he wasn't cruel enough to cut off his own children, was he? Luckily for Artem, it didn't matter—he had his own plans. He didn't want any more of his father's blood money, but he would use what he already had to get away. Hell, he'd earned it. And judging by the expression on his

siblings' faces, the sooner, the better. He just had
to—

"And that includes any money the three of you
think you've been so clever to hide."

He *knew*? But how? Artem's bank accounts were
supposed to be private—legally, anyway. Had his
father gotten one of his underlings to hack Artem's
accounts? Or had he simply paid yet another person
off? Artem could've slapped himself. Of course he
had. How could Artem have been stupid enough to
think otherwise? The dryness in his throat solidified,
choking him. He tried to hide his dismay, but he was
too slow.

"Yes, Artem, I know all about it. You can't do
anything without me knowing." Father shook his
head in disgust. "And you're supposed to be the
smart one."

"Hey—" Luka also rose.

"Oh, sit down, Luka."

He sat.

Coward.

But even Artem's mouth stayed shut, though his
mind screamed and beat itself against the inside of
his skull. *All those years of saving, of hiding. Of
hoping.* His throat was too dry to swallow. What
could he do now?

*You can still leave. You don't need him, or his
money.*

He weighed his options. He could get a job.
Somewhere far away from here. Somewhere beyond
his father's reach.

Where? Where could you possibly do that?

If they knew who his father was, they wouldn't
touch him with a ten-foot pole. And if they
didn't...his father would educate them sharply and

make them pay for their ignorance. Besides, what kind of job could he get? He didn't even have a formal education, for god's sake. His father had seen to that. Why waste time learning worldly nonsense when his only job was to be a dutiful son?

What about their family's competition? It would mean he'd have to hide from his father's rage for the rest of his life but...but it wouldn't work anyway. His father's mercurial reputation and refusal to adhere to any code of honor except his own meant that Artem was a no-go. If they didn't think he was a spy, they'd immediately try to use him as leverage against the Volkovs, and when they found out his family couldn't care less, they'd make him disappear. He'd have to find a different way. There had to *be* another way.

But in the end, his heart knew what his brain was trying to ignore. There was no escape.

And they all knew it.

As Father stared down at him, a triumphant smirk deepening the lines around his mouth, the desire to smash his plate over his father's head seized Artem again. Anything to break his composure, to make him react like the human he was supposed to be, rather than the soulless excuse for a person he insisted on being.

Artem had no choice. Each second he wasted trying to think of a way—any way—to get away from this, to slip his leash, he showed his hand. He had nothing. No power, nothing to bargain with but himself. And he wasn't worth anything to his father—at least, not until he *made* himself valuable. Only then might he be able to claw back the chance of freedom that was slipping away so quickly.

And there was only one way to do that—Artem

had to take on his father's mission.

He didn't want the business, or the money that came with it. But the power...that power, it would be his to control. He could use it to do whatever he wanted. He could put a muzzle on Paragon, make his father toothless. A voice in the back of his mind reminded him that his father would never give him that power, not really, but Artem pushed it down. He would find a way. Then he would use that power to take himself as far away from Portfade as he could and get a real life.

No matter how sour the taste it left in his mouth, he would have to play his father's game.

And he would have to win.

THREE

The air surrounding him felt thicker somehow, denser, as if the closely packed lifeforms had somehow pushed the molecules of oxygen closer together. Everything was different, damp and cool, the vegetal scent stirring some primordial awareness inside him. In only a few steps, Artem had passed from the light of the sun into the deep dusk of another world.

The Wildwood. Foxwept's very own haunted forest. The disaster that spawned it had happened when he was an adolescent, too wrapped up in his own world to care or even really notice. His family had money, so the mad scramble—for housing, food, basic healthcare—in the aftermath of the disaster hadn't affected him.

But now that he stood beyond the Perimeter, Artem understood. The fear those who'd lived here must've felt, the impotence. How could they ever have stood against such a force of nature? No wonder they'd been so grateful for the scratchy old blankets and expired rations they'd survived on during the evacuation. They'd witnessed the end of their world, an apocalypse that they'd escaped.

And those were just the people who'd left.

Everyone knew that people continued to live here,

but how could they stand it, having to carve themselves a niche in the ever-growing wilderness? Surely those who'd stayed behind had something seriously wrong with them—hardened criminals, perhaps, or those who were too ignorant to understand that people didn't have to live like animals.

And now he'd joined them, hoping to find a miracle in the mud.

At least getting in had been easier than he'd thought. An untraceable deposit chip to a disillusioned soldier was enough to turn his normally watchful eyes away, allowing him to pass unnoticed.

Well, almost.

As Artem had squeezed between trees growing so close together they seemed to form a wall, a single pair of eyes followed him. One of those droids, the non-sentient kind. They'd recently replaced the synadroids, sentient androids whose unexpected emotional responses had caused no end of trouble on the Perimeter. It stared after him, unmoving but for the turning of its head as it traced his path. It let him slink past, its expression bland and unconcerned. He shivered. Cold bastard. The droid knew he could be sneaking to his death.

He sighed. Time to start wandering about, looking for something, anything his mad king of a father could turn a quick buck on. But where to start? Everywhere he looked was a tangle of green. He cocked his head, listening. Perhaps if he could hear running water, he could find something to follow, to give him some bearings. But there was nothing, the heavy silence not lightened even by the sound of birds. He was surrounded by life, yet there was no movement, nothing, as if the entire place was holding its breath, as though it believed if it were silent and still enough, the intruder would leave.

Artem shook himself.

Stop thinking about it as though it's alive. Do that, and you'll lose your mind before you find anything useful.

Seriously, though, what the hell is with these plants? He'd heard strange stories about the Wildwood from people who'd ventured beyond the border on some kind of botanical joyride—or who at least knew someone who knew someone who had. They told crazy tales of mutated animals, monstrous plants, and even a house that disappeared and reappeared at will. He hadn't really believed any of it, but looking around him now, it seemed the stories had been conservative at best.

The ground in front of him was deeply carpeted with strange plants—fleshy, luminescent mushrooms; tall, flat grasses that were paper-thin and veined like dragonfly wings; thin, red stems holding clusters of white berries that—oh my god, were they eyeballs? He tried to swallow past the sudden tightness in his throat. *No.* It couldn't be.

It's just part of the plant.

A marking. But as he backed away, his skin crawling, he swore the tiny eyes followed him accusingly, berating him for trespassing.

There was a rustling in the undergrowth behind him, and he spun, his heart picking up in a wild rhythm. What now? He'd been in here for less than an hour; surely, he could make it longer than that?

Long enough to find something to beat Luka and Misha at least.

What would his father do if none of them came back? Would the mad bastard have the balls to come here himself? Would he even look for them?

I mean, what kind of father would willingly put his children in danger?

A face poked out of the underbrush. Two faces. On one neck. Crowned with three long ears that were flicking back and forth.

Bile rose in his throat. The creature before him was a caricature of the rabbits ubiquitous throughout Foxwept. Its noses twitched and whiskers quivered as it sniffed the air, tasting him.

Was it dangerous?

Just walk away.

He turned as quietly as he could, stepping gingerly over the roots snaking across the ground. The rabbit-thing was almost out of sight when his ankle caught on something and he crashed to the ground, landing flat on his back with the wind knocked out of him.

Was it just his imagination or was the monster rabbit laughing at him? He rolled over and a warm wetness seeped into the front of his shirt. And the *smell. Oh my god.* He scrambled to his feet and looked down in horror. A thick substance was smeared across the front of his shirt—his *designer* shirt. From the stain rose the scent of burned hair, of rotted flesh, of— Artem gagged. Tiny shreds of what looked like pale green skin clung to the fabric over his chest. Whatever he'd rolled over was alive...or at least, it had been.

He pressed the back of his hand to his mouth. Son of a b—

The rabbit was definitely laughing at him.

It was the last straw. No matter what he did, what he found, even if he came home victorious, he would still smell like failure. He could just picture his father's face, the curl of his lip as he shook his head in disgust. It wouldn't matter how valuable Artem's information was; the victory wouldn't be clean, wouldn't be *perfect*. Wouldn't be enough. The sheer unfairness of it all overwhelmed him and he let out a long string of curses. He advanced on the rabbit, even though he had no idea what he would do if he actually caught it. He didn't have to worry, though, because it melted into the dense brush before he could get close. The ease with which the little animal navigated the tangle infuriated him. He bent and snatched a rock from the ground and threw it as hard as he could in the direction the creature had gone.

Ha, take that, freak.

There was a strangled cry as it hit its mark, and his anger dissipated as quickly as it had come.

He turned, about to head off in the opposite direction when it occurred to him. Maybe *this* was what he'd been looking for. Maybe there was an untapped market for freaky mutant animals. All the rich people he knew were into weird stuff—the more exotic, the better. He pushed through the undergrowth, touching as little of the surrounding foliage as he could. With any luck, the wretched thing would be dead, and he could just bag it up and head home. If his father thought it had potential, he could send in some of his cronies to capture an entire herd of the bizarre little bastards. Job done. If he snuck in the side door, he might be able to make it to his room without anyone smelling him. A quick shower and a change of clothes, and he could be sitting with his feet up, savoring his victory and a glass of lucéat when Luka and Misha finally staggered in.

With a last big push, he broke through the overgrown tangle and into a small clearing.

Crap.

His rock had struck home all right. A figure lay crumpled on the ground, his rock by its head.

Only, it wasn't a two-headed rabbit.

Instead, there was a young woman with long red hair that spread out from her pale face like a blanket over the ground, a thin line of blood oozing slowly from her temple. If it hadn't been for her flaming hair and pale face, he might've stepped on her, so well did she blend with the forest around her. She wore a long skirt subtly stippled like the copses around her. Her t-shirt was nothing more than simple brown cotton, her boots a sturdy-looking leather in a similar tan.

"Hello?" She didn't move. He nudged her with his toes. "Are you okay?" She didn't *look* okay.

What in blazes was she doing in the Wildwood? Did she live here? He crouched next to her. Surely not. She didn't look like a miscreant or some backwoods rube. Her simple clothes were worn but unsoiled. Her hair was shiny and her face clean. She must be some kind of runaway then, escaping from god-knew-what only to be bashed in the head the moment she'd finally found her freedom. Great. Now the bad luck that seemed to have plagued Artem his whole life was spreading and infecting other people.

Was she dead? His mind raced. What should he do?

If his father were here, he would've insisted on leaving her, would've said it was a hazard of choosing to live in such a place. *Play stupid games, win stupid prizes.*

But Artem wasn't his father. He may have been here at his behest, but Artem drew the line way above leaving people for dead. So what to do?

He leaned forward and placed his hand on her chest, trying to see if it rose and fell. But he couldn't be sure. Maybe if he—

Something snapped the air right next to his head, barely missing his scalp. He threw himself backward, crab-crawling over the uneven ground, dirt piling under his fingernails. *What the—*

A huge plant strained toward him, its massive jaws biting at empty space. It paused, its wide mouth partly open as if it was trying to figure out where its prey had gone.

You have got *to be kidding.*

The abomination looked like it wanted to swallow him whole, and he didn't doubt for a second that it could.

As though it sensed Artem was no longer in its range, it pulled back, lowering its dripping maw toward the prone woman.

Could it reach her? If she wasn't already dead, would it finish her off?

Artem didn't want to find out. It was one thing to have accidentally hit her with a rock, another to sit by and actually watch her get eaten by some monstrous shrub.

Swearing, he leaped to his feet and darted over to her, wrapping his hands as securely around her glove-clad wrists as he could. The plant quivered at the sudden movement and sprang, its jaws impossibly wide. The barbed lips narrowly missed Artem's shoulder as he dragged the young woman out of its reach as quickly as he could. Her skirt caught on something and tore, but still Artem pulled, until finally, they were out of range. He sank to the ground, gasping for breath.

This place was crazy, a world unto itself, and so

much more than Artem had bargained for. He'd been here...what, less than a couple of hours? And already he'd been covered in fetid slime, laughed at by a two-headed bunny, *and* nearly eaten by a carnivorous flower. *Forget this.* He'd just suck it up and let his father cast him out.

The weight of the woman's head on his leg brought his attention back to her. At least he'd managed to save her. *If* she was still alive, of course.

He whipped his transcomm out of his pocket. He would call Loth, ask for his help. God knew he'd gotten Loth out of more than one sticky situation; his friend owed him.

But he wasn't going to be calling anyone. The signal bar on his comm didn't even register, the words 'no signal' blinking infuriatingly at him, mocking him. Seriously? No comm service? It just got better and better. Now what? Should he stand in the middle of the clearing screaming for help until someone finally came looking? Should he try to pick her up and carry her out to the line of soldiers?

Or you could just dump her close enough for them to find her, the devil of his father whispered in his ear. *No need to waste any more time.*

If that was what Father would've done, he definitely wasn't going to do that.

Right. Think. He stared down at her still-motionless form. *First of all, make sure she's alive.*

He pressed two fingers to her neck. Was that her pulse? He wasn't quite sure; the pounding of blood in his own ears was too distracting. Nor could he tell if her chest was rising and falling with breath, or if he simply hoped it was. What about her wrists? He could try checking her pulse there.

He lifted one of her arms. Her hand was encased

in a glove of some kind of stretchy black mesh. Definitely not an ordinary glove. Above the cuff was a wound, previously hidden by her hair. A row of deep punctures, with angry red veins all the way up to her shoulder. Was it from that terrible plant? It had to be.

He couldn't feel her pulse through her gloves, so he peeled one off then turned her hand over, his fingers hovering over her wrist.

It took him a second to understand what he was seeing then another for his brain to engage enough to command his body to scramble back, to get away.

Her hand. What's the matter with her hand?

It was worse than the rabbit, worse than the plant. This place was wrong, the forest and everything in it. None of it should've been able to exist.

Not plants with eyes, animals with too many faces, and *especially* not women with the hands of frogs.

FOUR

Why was her head throbbing? And what was she doing on the ground? Lissa's mind worked slowly and painfully back, trying to remember. Swift. The corpselure. She'd been reaching inside to scoop up some of the sap when… She raised her hand to her head, and her fingers came away slick with blood. Something had struck her, that was clear, but what?

And why was one of her gloves off? She tried to sit up, but the spinning of the Wildwood all around her gleefully forbade it. She counted slowly to ten then tried again, this time easing herself up slowly.

A young man crouched about a dozen feet away from her, poised as though about to run. His tanned face was pale, not the sun-starved paleness of her own complexion, but the ivory of shock. His mouth was twisted into an ugly grimace and his gaze was pinned to her hand.

Her hand. Naked, it rested on the ground, her fingers splayed, the webbing stretched between them delicate and iridescent. And completely inhuman. Monstrous even, if the way he was looking at her was any indication. She fought the urge to hide them behind her back.

It had been a long time since anyone had looked at her like that. The Goldhare disaster had left its mark on everyone in the now-Wildwood. Though hers was more extreme than most, differences like Lissa's were just a fact of life for many people, one they accepted in each other. Those outside the Wildwood were another matter, and the man's scowl of disgust reminded her exactly why she avoided leaving this sanctuary whenever she could.

Then his eyes met hers and he shrank back even further, pressing himself against the bark of a thick, gnarled tree. Still she refused to look away. She had her pride, after all, even if his reaction had completely shredded her dignity. Judging by his expensive clothes, the insolent set of his shoulders, the exaggerated horror on his face, he was clearly not of the Wildwood, and there was no way she would be shamed in her own home, not by someone like *him*. She resisted the urge to spit on the ground, to expel the bitter taste his people left in her mouth. Swift argued that her eyes—the unmistakably amphibian marquise shape of her pupil, the otherworldly gold and green-ringed iris—were one of her best features, and despite her mortification about them, there was no way she was going to let some pasty-faced ass from the city make her blink.

He looked away first.

"Who are you? What are you doing here?" It came out gruffer than she'd intended, but his kind always rankled.

He looked up at her again then dropped his gaze almost as quickly.

He can't even bear to look at me. Shame curled her fingers into the dirt, the pressure under her nails an anchor. "Well?"

He raised his eyes again and, this time, held her gaze. His own eyes were the rich, dark brown of fertile earth, one of her favorite colors. Too bad they were in *his* head. "I— I was walking and I— I'm so sorry. I threw a rock, and I think I hit you." He gestured to her head, which was still throbbing.

"You threw a rock at me?"

"No! I mean, yes, but not on purpose. I meant to hit a rabbit...a rabbit with two faces, and I—"

"You were trying to hit a dyahare? Why would you do that? They're completely harmless!"

"Two faces. It had *two faces*." He held up two fingers as though she didn't know what the word "two" meant.

"So?"

"*So?* You say that like it's normal."

She shrugged. "It is." How were people like him, supposedly educated and cosmopolitan, still so ignorant?

"Seriously? *I've* never heard—" He narrowed his eyes. "Are you okay?"

She wasn't. As he spoke, her vision blurred and the world started to spin again. What was happening? Was the knock on her head worse than she'd thought? She raised her hand to touch it again and caught sight of her arm, the holes in her skin and the red tracks darkening to a dusky purple.

Venom. She'd been envenomed by the corpselure when it bit her. She clawed at her pocket, trying to get hold of the small ampoule that held the antidote. Where was it? Had it fallen out? She lurched over onto her hands and knees and ran her fingers over the ground.

"Are you okay?" he repeated, his voice coming from far away.

I have to take the antidote before the venom reaches my brain. But all that came out was "I have…venom."

"What?" The voice came closer, throbbing in pitch, in her ear one minute, then the other side of the world the next. The stippled light coming through the canopy strobed in time to the throbbing of her own heart as it tried to force itself from her chest. A face appeared above her, a young man, his golden skin bathed in a halo of light. His eyes shone with concern, and his lips seemed to be moving, speaking to her, and they were so full and soft that all she needed to do before she died was reach out and touch them, just once—

Swift. The tiny part of her that the venom hadn't yet reached, the part of her that had always resolutely survived, screamed at her. *Swift.* She fumbled in her pocket for the device he'd given her. If she could just press the button, just…press.

Sound no longer came from those beautiful lips, though they continued to move in a hypnotic rhythm over her, giving her last rites.

A new strength found her hand and she pressed the button.

A whisper spread from her then, rippling through the surrounding plants in an ever-widening sigh. There. Now she could give up, give in. Next time, he could get his own stupid sap. His own…

She rose, flying, despite the heaviness of her arms and legs. Over the ground she sailed, bright and hot one minute as she flew close to the sun, cool and heavy as she flowed through the depth of the ocean before landing in her final resting place, somewhere soft and warm, and infused with the scent of sage.

FIVE

"Are you okay? Are you—" As the young woman's eyelids fluttered and she sank to the ground, Artem tried to push her webbed hands and disturbing eyes to the back of his mind. Whatever that plant had done to her, she was in trouble. She'd said something about venom. Did it have anything to do with those terrible marks on her arm?

What am I supposed to do?

He'd never learned any first aid, had never thought he'd need to. He leaned over her, hoping she'd be able to hear him as she slipped in and out of consciousness. "Can you hear me? What do you mean you've been envenomed?"

She didn't reply, and he cursed himself. It didn't matter what had happened, he just needed to know what to do. After all, he couldn't just leave her, could he?

Sure you can, Father's voice rasped in his mind. *The freak is not your problem. Just walk away and get on with it.*

For a moment, he was sorely tempted. The thought of accidentally touching those hands... He shuddered.

She seemed to be fumbling in the pocket of her long skirt, as though she were looking for something.

Should he try to get it for her? But as he reached for her pocket, his fears came true as their hands touched. He recoiled, yanking his back. He'd expected her fingers to be moist and clammy, like the skin of a frog, and instead, they were warm and soft. But the webbing between her fingers... He just couldn't. Nausea roiled in his stomach as the toxic voice of his father leaked unbidden into his mind again.

Just walk away. Given what she is, it's better that way...

No.

The voice galvanized him. Whatever else this woman was, she was still a human being, and there was no way he would let her die. His family had enough on their consciences.

Her fingers had closed around something in her pocket, but she was too weak now to withdraw it. Artem took a deep breath and slipped his hand into the folds of fabric to help her, trying not to think about the slide of her skin against his. Grasped in her fingers was a small device.

Some kind of nanocomm.

If it was, they were in trouble. If he couldn't get a signal on one of the best transcomms on the market...

Still, it was the only chance they had. Her finger hovered over a small button on the side, pushing at it feebly. He put his finger over hers and pressed it hard for good measure. For a moment, the space around the device seemed to waver like the haze over a fire, and Artem swore he felt a disturbance in the air, though it was gone before he could be sure. The plants around them seemed to feel it too, rustling and bending as though whispering amongst themselves.

Now what? Could he carry her out of here?

He bent and scooped her up in his arms; she was lighter than he'd expected. Her long hair hung nearly to the ground even as he tried to nudge her head to rest on his shoulder. Shining like burnished copper, it smelled faintly of rain and some kind of flower that tickled the back of his mind, softening everything around him. His eyelids grew heavy, and he wanted nothing more than to close them, to sink to the ground and—

The forest around him shuddered and the massive plants bent slightly, as though making way for something. The fog in his brain vanished as footsteps, heavy and deliberate, came straight for him.

Cold fear darted through him. Could he run with her in his arms? The ground was so uneven, an open invitation to a twisted ankle...and to make matters worse, he had no idea where he was. He'd gotten turned around when he'd gone searching for the twin-faced rabbit. For all he knew, he would just be running deeper and deeper into the Wildwood, into the hungry mouth of—

A creature burst from the trees, and Artem nearly dropped his cargo.

What the blazing hell is that?

It looked like... But it couldn't be. A story came to him then, told to him and his friends by one of their governesses. At the time, he'd assumed she'd had one too many glasses of lucéat, painting a wild tale for them about a house that wandered the Wildwood on legs of animal bone. Although, looking at its legs, he couldn't imagine what animal they could possibly have come from. Spiders simply didn't grow that big. Or have bones, for that matter.

These legs were long and spindly, thicker in circumference than his body. Alternating in pairs as they marched along, they moved with an arachnid grace that made him want to throw up.

Please, please let it be manmade, whatever it is.

If there truly were spiders that big, with bones, in the Wildwood, he was done. His father could do whatever he liked to him; he was never coming back here, not even if his life depended on it.

But what about her? Artem glanced down at the woman in his arms. Dropping her and running wasn't an option, despite every nerve in his body screaming at him to do just that. No, he would stand his ground. There was no way he'd be able to outrun whatever it was anyway. He took a deep breath and waited.

Atop the hideous legs was what appeared to be a house. *Bunty was telling the truth. If I get out of here alive, I'm going to make sure Nate and Loth never tease her again.*

The house was made from dark wood, disturbingly traditional in contrast to its macabre foundation. With window boxes stuffed with a profusion of wildflowers and carved lattices adorning every edge and corner, it looked like any of the quaint holiday cottages Artem had stayed in when he was younger and his father was still attempting the charade of quality family time.

A balcony sat above the front door of the cottage, and standing on it, clutching the railing was a person, their long silver hair swaying in time with the house's steps. Artem's heart nearly stopped in his chest as the house came to a halt in front of him. The figure on the balcony barked a command in a distinctly male voice, and the house folded its legs beneath itself, curling them inward until the door stood only a few feet off the ground. A set of stairs slid out from under the frame and clattered down, but the man on the balcony ignored them, leaping from the second story and sprinting toward them the minute his feet touched the earth.

"Lissa!" His eyes were wild as he snatched the woman away from Artem and knocked him roughly with his shoulder, sending Artem staggering back. "What did you do to her?"

Artem raised his hands in surrender. "I was trying to help her. Before she passed out, she said something about venom. She's got some kind of bite mark on her arm—" A bite mark that had nothing to do with his rock, thankfully.

"A bite?" The man looked sharply at Artem, laid the young woman—Lissa, he'd called her—gently onto the ground, and knelt beside her.

"It's her left arm." He wanted to help but didn't dare take another step closer. This man commanded a walking house, for goodness' sake. Artem was fine where he was.

The man lifted the lengths of hair lying over Lissa's arm and swore. "Oh, Lissa, how did this happen?" He glared up at Artem. "The antidote, do you have it?"

Artem shook his head. "I don't know anything about an antidote. When I found her, she'd already been…bitten, or whatever happened." Even from where he stood, the severity of her injury was obvious, the tracks up her arm now an inky, evil-looking black.

The stranger bent back over her and ran his hands over her body. "Damnit, Lissa, don't tell me you went without the antidote." His hands stopped moving suddenly and he turned to glare up at Artem. "Stay right there. I mean it. Don't you dare move from that spot." He sprinted back to the cottage and disappeared inside, only to fly out moments later clutching a tiny ampoule. He bit off the top of the small vial and forced his fingers into her mouth before pouring the contents down her throat.

She gagged and tried to cough the liquid out, but he clamped her jaw shut and held it, as her hands clawed at his.

Then only a few seconds later, Lissa stopped fighting, her body limp. Was she dead? "Is she—"

The man turned on him. "What did you do to her?"

"Nothing! Like I told you, she'd been bitten by the time I reached her."

"I don't believe you. She's careful. She knows the risks—" His eyes flashed with a weird, inhuman light. "You must have done *something*."

Maybe it was time to confess. Artem was in a vulnerable position here. If she woke up and told this man what had happened, and he realized Artem had lied... Besides, it *had* been an accident. "I may have hit her with a rock. On the head." He winced. It sounded much worse when he said it out loud. What was this guy going to do to him?

He stared at Artem with such ferocity the hair on the back of his neck stood up. "You hit her? With a rock?" He bared his teeth.

"It was an accident. I was trying to hit something else, and—"

"And you must've distracted her," the man finished. "Do you have any idea what you've done?" His voice rose and the forest seemed to crowd closer around them. "How could you have been so stupid?

She could've died!"

Could have? Did that mean she was going to be okay?

The stranger launched himself at Artem, knocking him to the ground. His momentum sent them rolling painfully over exposed roots and rocks, and something that squished in a way Artem would remember for the rest of his life.

Artem swung wildly, trying to land a blow wherever he could. Normally he could take down opponents twice his size, but this one was too fast, with a wily strength that rained down strikes thick and fast on Artem's face and shoulders. Out of the corner of his eye, he saw Lissa stagger to her feet.

She's alive.

His rival took advantage of his distraction and landed a heavy punch square on his temple, and as his head snapped back, he swore the trees were laughing. It was the last weirdness in an unbearably surreal day. Was anything he'd seen even real? Maybe he'd been bitten by some kind of crazy, mutated mosquito the minute he crossed the Perimeter and was hallucinating every single moment of this.

The ground was so soft as he sank into it, the whirling of the forest around him cradling him in its vortex. Warmth suffused his limbs and a peace he hadn't felt in years came over him.

Maybe this place isn't so bad. Maybe...

SIX

"You didn't have to hit him so hard, you know." Lissa wrung as much cold water from the cloth as she could before laying it across the young man's forehead. Still, a cold trickle ran down his face and soaked into the pillow Swift had placed under his head.

"We would've been rolling around all day if I hadn't. Besides, what difference does it make? He's just some townie who's got no business being here. And, in case you forgot, he hit you with a *rock*, Lissa. He could've killed you."

"Stop being so melodramatic. I'm fine." True, her head was still throbbing, but no permanent damage had been done. "Besides, at least he didn't get me *envenomed*. If anything was going to kill me today, it would've been that."

Swift flinched. "Lissa, I'm so sorry. I never—"

"Swift, I'm joking." Now that the danger was over, she wasn't mad at him. "I knew the risk when I agreed to get the sap for you."

"I know, but if you'd been hurt—" He wrapped his arms around her, pulling her close to his chest. "I don't know what I would've done if I'd lost you. You're my…well, you're everything to me." He laid his chin on the top of her head and sighed.

"Yeah? Well, next time come with me then." She punched him playfully on the shoulder, and he released her with a grin.

"How *is* your arm?" A dark shadow passed over his face as he examined her for what seemed like the hundredth time.

She pulled it away. "It's fine, seriously. Stop worrying about it." She was still a little light-headed from the venom that had coursed through her veins, and her arm still bore its insidious marks, but they were fading fast. She'd spend the night at Swift's just to make sure, and to keep her mother from asking too many questions. Mom trusted her to be sensible out in the wild, and Lissa didn't want to give her a reason not to.

She bent over their guest. "I wonder what he was doing out here." A foul odor rose from him, and she gagged. "What is that smell?"

Swift leaned over and sniffed. "Niff-mantid." He snorted. "I hope he likes it, because that smell is never coming out."

"Shouldn't we...do something about it?"

"Like?"

"I don't know, take off his shirt?"

"Or we could just send him home with a souvenir."

"Swift!" Just because his kind usually treated people like Lissa like dung on the bottom of their shoes didn't mean they had to stoop to the same level, no matter how tempting it might be.

"Oh fine. Do you want me to do the honors?"

Did she? Part of her wanted to touch the expensive fabric, to feel it slide between her fingers as she peeled it up over his chest. Her hands might brush that tanned, satiny skin. What would it feel like? Skin protected from the dangers and poverty of the Wildwood? Her mouth went dry. What was she thinking? He was just another spoiled brat from Portfade, out slumming in the Wildwood so he could brag about it to his rich friends.

"Yeah, you do it." She pressed the back of her hand to her nose. "What *do* you think he was doing here?"

Swift snorted and echoed her thoughts. "Probably on some dare from his friends. You know how they get. 'Run and touch a tree in the haunted forest!' Idiots." He yanked the shirt over the man's head so roughly his head bounced on the table.

"Be careful!" The more she thought about it, the less it seemed like a joyride visit. He'd come prepared for something more than a dare, if his gear was anything to go by. In the trees next to the clearing, they'd found a backpack filled with various survival gear, all new. No, he was definitely here for a reason. But what?

She tried to avoid looking at his now-bare chest but failed miserably. He had the lean muscles of an active and obscenely healthy and well-fed young man. His skin was the same golden tan as his face, smooth and unmarked. She leaned closer. "How old do you think he is?" He had to be close to her age, perhaps a little older. Maybe nineteen or twenty?

"He'll be awake soon, and then you can ask him. Or do you think we should just meander over to the Perimeter and drop him off? Let the soldiers find him?" Swift crossed his arms over his chest. "If you want my opinion, I think that's the best idea. Let him wake up and think this was all a dream."

It was probably the right thing to do. But... Lissa was reluctant to get rid of the stranger yet. "He did try to help me. I should at least thank him. Plus, the soldiers have enough on their hands without having to cart some rich kid back to the right side of the Perimeter."

Swift shrugged. "Suit yourself."

The stranger's eyelids fluttered, and he murmured something too quiet to hear.

Swift narrowed his eyes. "Actually, I think he's waking up."

Lissa stepped back to give him some space. The color had returned to his tanned face, giving him a golden, robust look rarely seen in the Wildwood. His mouth was curved even in sleep, like a mouth that smiled often and generously. His expensively cut hair was a rich brown, straight and impossibly glossy, close-cropped on the sides and back, but long enough to graze his lips on top. His hands were soft and uncalloused, unlike any she'd seen before. Next to him, she and Swift looked practically feral.

He stirred, mumbling a little to himself again before falling still. Had it been a false alarm? "Maybe he just—"

He shot up, his eyes wide, his head whipping from side to side before he tried to scramble off the pallet, his legs tangling in the blanket Swift had laid over him and sending him crashing to the floor. The entire house shuddered, and Lissa swore Swift bit back a laugh.

"What— Where am I?" He looked down at himself. "Where's my shirt?"

"You murdered a niff-mantid at some point during your adventure." Swift smiled blandly. "The smell was making us sick."

The man winced and touched the side of his head. "Why do I have such a bad headache?"

Swift smiled again. "I knocked you out."

The man's eyes narrowed as he tried to remember. He caught sight of Lissa standing behind Swift's shoulder and nodded slowly. "I remember now. He, your—" He pointed at Swift.

"Friend." Why had she said that?

Her embarrassment deepened as he shrugged dismissively—he obviously couldn't have cared less about the relationship between her and Swift. "Your *friend* thought I'd done something to you."

Swift stared at him. "You *did.* You hit her in the head with a rock."

The man gave Lissa a glib smile. "I did. It was an accident. Sorry." He shook his head, any concern for her well-being squared away. "What the hell *was* that thing? That plant?"

"A corpselure. They have sap that—"

The silver-haired man interrupted her. "Who are you?"

"My name's Artem." His smile at Lissa was perfunctory, the kind you gave a stranger in passing.

Lissa had thought her embarrassment couldn't get any worse, but he wasn't even looking at her. Despite his attempt at discretion, his line of sight skimmed just past her ear, avoiding her face altogether. Her face, with the eyes he obviously found repulsive. Shame bloomed warmly in her cheeks as it always did. It disappeared quickly under the rush of anger that followed, but the seed had sprouted, the precursor to a vicious weed she was exhausted trying to uproot. Swift was right. This man, whatever he was up to, was trouble. She narrowed her eyes at him.

Artem cleared his throat awkwardly and glanced around. "Where's my bag?"

Swift pointed to the corner. "There."

"Did you, uh, look through it?"

Swift crossed his arms over his chest. "Why? Hiding something?"

Artem gave a flippant shrug. "Of course not." There was a challenge in his voice, as though he was daring Swift to upend his bag and rifle through it.

Lissa almost snorted. He had no business being here, and yet he was acting as though *they* were the intruders. His arrogance was admirable.

Swift cocked his head. "What are you doing here? In the Wildwood?"

Artem shrugged. "Hiking."

Hiking? Seriously? Lissa couldn't bite back her laugh in time.

Artem looked sharply at her. "What? Why's that so funny?"

"Because we *did* look through your pack. And everything in it, plus the boots on your feet, is brand-new. You've never been hiking in your life."

A muscle in his face twitched as emotions played across it—anger, embarrassment, self-consciousness—and it gave her a perverse thrill of delight. But it didn't last. He shrugged, his composure back. "Well, today seemed like a good day to start."

He was insufferable. And yet, despite herself, the tiniest beginning of a smile quirked the corner of her mouth. What was wrong with her? He was exactly the kind of man her mother had warned her about, from one of the wealthy Portfade families who looked at everyone else—and those in the Wildwood especially—as disposable. She was nothing but trash to him. Mutant trash. He still couldn't look her in the eye.

"Would you like something to drink?" The words were out of her mouth before she knew they were coming.

Swift glared at her, irritation rolling off him in near-tangible waves. "I'm sure he has to get going, Liss," he said pointedly. "Not many hours of sunlight left for his *hike*."

The intruder leaned back, making himself at home. "Actually, I'd love something to drink."

Swift shot daggers at Lissa as he slammed a cup of tepid water down in front of Artem. "Here. Enjoy." He raised an eyebrow, daring an objection.

Artem downed the contents in one gulp. "Thank you. That was delicious." He put the cup down gracefully, as though it were precious china. He pointed to the various dried herbs hanging from the rafters. "What are those?"

"Plants."

He waited for Swift to say more. When he didn't, Artem turned to Lissa for help. And stopped. "Hey, what happened to your head?"

"You hit it with a rock."

He at least had the decency to look sheepish. "Yes, I know that. But it's healed. I mean, there was a cut there before, wasn't there?"

"Yes."

"How?" There was an odd intensity to his gaze. Why was he so interested? Warning bells went off in her mind, echoed by Swift making a low sound in his throat.

He's one of them.

They came every year, though less and less as the people of the Wildwood learned to identify them and close ranks accordingly. Men and women coming into the mysterious jungle, hoping to find the next big thing—whether a new flower, or exotic animal, or miracle cure—to sell to the highest bidder, flooding the sanctuary of the Wildwood with those more than happy to exploit it, stripping it bare for whatever profit they could get. Laws had been passed early on making it illegal to remove any plant or animal material from the Wildwood in order to prevent it spreading, but that didn't deter everyone.

Lissa kept her expression neutral. "It was a superficial cut. You need to work on your throwing arm." But Lissa wasn't in the habit of lying, and her eyes flicked involuntarily to the table in the corner where Swift made his concoctions. She tore them away almost in the same instant, but it was clear from the cunning expression on his handsome face that he'd seen exactly what she'd been looking at. *Damn him.*

He was a bit too willing to let it go. "Yeah, I'll do that. Not much call for it where I come from. Though I can see why it would be useful *here*."

Anger burned through her. *Arrogant ass.* She picked his niff-mantid-soaked shirt off the floor where Swift had dropped it and chucked it at him. It hit him on the chest and stuck with a satisfying plop. There. Much better.

He leaped up and the shirt fell to the floor. Reddish-brown, foul-smelling slime was plastered to his skin, and Lissa had never smelled a stench as sweet. "Hey! What are you doing?"

"I thought you'd like your shirt back. I mean, you can't go hiking with all that skin on display." She raised an eyebrow at him. "You might get mistaken for something's lunch. Something with much better aim than you."

His mouth twisted and a shadow passed over his

face.

Good. Let him feel off-balance for once in his life.
Then, to her surprise, he laughed and held up his hands. "Okay, I surrender. I'm sorry. I shouldn't be here, I know that."

"Then why are you here?"

"Honestly? I...just wanted to see something different. I get tired of seeing the same things day after day."

Swift choked back a sarcastic laugh. "Diamond shoes too tight, are they?"

Artem shrugged. "I don't expect you to understand. And I'm okay with that. You asked and I'm just being honest. I know I look like a fool to you, and maybe I am."

Why the quick about-face in attitude? Could he simply be telling the truth? *If so, I know exactly how he feels.* Clearly, he had every material advantage that could be had in Portfade, but maybe that did grow stagnant after a while. *I mean, my life here in the Wildwood is pretty good. We're lucky compared to many, and I'd still like to see other things.*

Swift wasn't convinced. "At the end of the day, it doesn't matter why you're here. What *does* matter is what you're going to do now."

"Now?"

Swift spoke slowly, as though to a child. "Yes. Now. See that big, bright ball in the sky? It's going to go down in the next couple of hours, and then you're going to see something different all right, something more than you bargained for. No amount of fancy gear in the world is going to help your ignorant ass then."

"Can't I stay here? I can pay you."

Swift's mouth dropped open. It was obviously the

last thing he'd expected. "Do I look like a hotel to you?" He pointed toward the door. "Out. Now."

"Swi—"

He rounded on Lissa. "He's not staying here."

"I'm not saying that. I—" She was acutely aware that Artem could hear every word she said. "Can we...go outside for a moment?" She gave the tiniest nod in Artem's direction.

Swift threw up his hands in exasperation. "Of course. God forbid we hurt his feelings by talking in front of him."

What was up with Swift today? He could be salty at the best of times, but he was being unusually prickly. True, he couldn't stand strangers, and spoiled men-children like Artem were right up there on his list of hates, but he usually put on at least the pretense of tolerance. Well, he'd only have to bear Artem for a little while longer.

They walked down the stairs and a few yards from the house. Swift crossed his arms over his chest. "Well?"

"Well...what *are* we going to do with him? I know he can't stay here," she rushed on, as he opened his mouth to protest. "But we can't let him wander around the Wildwood in the dark either."

"Why not?"

"Because— You know why not, Swift. He'll never survive out here."

"So? They need to learn. People like him...they can't keep coming here. They don't belong here, Lissa. They have no right to be here."

"But I know what it's like to want to get away—"

"You didn't actually believe that, did you?" He gave a brittle laugh. "Lissa, come on. How could you? He just wants to see the world?" He whipped his hand toward the house. "His kind *owns* the world. You think he can't go jetting off whenever he wants, wherever he wants?" He dropped his gaze. "Why are you so bothered about him anyway?"

Heat rose into Lissa's face. This wasn't going the way she'd wanted it to—but what *had* she wanted?

I just want to make sure he's safe...because it's the right thing to do, nothing else.

Why did Swift think it was anything but that?

"I'm not. It's just, if something happened to him, do you really want that on your conscience?" Of course he didn't. Swift was a lot of things but heartless wasn't one of them.

He looked closely at her. "Is that the *real* reason? You've never worried about my conscience before." His tone was stiff and there was a new coolness between them.

"I just...look, if something happens to him, don't you think his family is going to come looking for him? Is that what you want? Dozens of them crawling over the Wildwood?"

"Of course not."

"Well, then?"

Swift groaned. "Fine. But one night only, okay? One night. As soon as the sun rises tomorrow morning, he's out of here, yes?"

"Yes. I promise."

"And you'll stay too? I can't promise what I might do if you leave me alone with him."

"Of course I'll stay." She threw her arms around him, confused by the relief rushing through her. "Thanks, Swift. I know it's a big ask."

He pressed his lips to her hair. "You owe me."

She snorted. "Let's call it even for the corpselure,

okay?"

Warm breath whooshed into her scalp as he laughed. "Okay."

She climbed the stairs first. "Good news, Artem. Swift has agreed to let you stay. It's just for the night, but—"

He was standing in the middle of the room, his pack on his shoulders.

"You're leaving?"

"Yes. I'm sorry. I've taken up enough of your time and hospitality already."

"But you can't be out in the Wildwood after the sun goes down. It's too dangerous. There are things that—" Why was she babbling? And trying to keep him here? If he wanted to go, let him. They'd done what they could by offering him a place to stay. They couldn't force him to take it.

He smiled, the infuriatingly attractive dimple in his cheek causing an odd ache in her chest. "That's so kind of you, especially after what I did."

"Don't worry about it."

"No really. I am sorry. I know I was a huge pain in the ass. I'll get out of your way." He looked at her then, really looked at her. In the eyes. And he didn't flinch.

In truth, she was torn. He *was* a giant pain in the ass. But if he left, she might never see him again.

Why do you want to? Just because he smiled at you? When did your standards get so low?

It was more than that, but with him looking at her and the twisting in her stomach, she couldn't figure it out.

"Well, you're more self-aware than I'd have given you credit for, so that's something." Swift leaned against the doorway, his gaze passing between them.

Artem looked away. "I'm glad to hear I'm not all bad." He nodded to Lissa as she stepped out of the way. "I'm not going to stay in the Wildwood. I'm going home. You were right— I don't belong here." He rearranged his pack on his shoulders. "If you two could just point me in the right direction?"

Swift glanced at Lissa then scrubbed his hands over his face. "How about we take you close to the Perimeter? We can show you the way from there. It won't take long."

Artem gave a curt nod. "Thanks."

An hour later, the orange sun darkened and began to sink, and shadows stretched across the Wildwood. Night in the Wood was as beautiful as it was deadly, and already its splendor stirred in Lissa's bones. Perhaps they would go to the lagoon tonight, and watch the lights swooping out over the water from the safety of Swift's cottage. They would eat smoked honey and talk and laugh and make fun of Artem and people like him and pretend he'd never made them feel less than they were.

Swift's cursing brought Lissa out of her reverie.

She joined him at the control room window on the upper floor. "What?"

"The soldiers are further in than normal. I'm not sure how we're going to get him any closer and not be seen ourselves."

Lissa chewed on her thumb. They were still too deep in the woods to let Artem out here, but Swift was right—the soldiers seeing them, Hedwig in particular, was an even greater risk.

"What about the doorway?" The residents of the forest used the tunnel running under the Perimeter when they wanted to cross from the Wood to the rest of Foxwept Province. That it was a closely guarded secret was an unspoken rule.

Swift was already shaking his head. "No way. We can't, Liss. What if he tells someone?"

"Who would care? Besides, people can get past the soldiers anyway. *He* did," she reminded him.

"Yes, but that's different. That's on them. The doorway is on *us*."

"It's not like he'd ever be able to find it again." She meant it; the doorway was hard to find on both sides, even if you were looking for it.

Swift pressed his lips together in a thin line. "Fine." He tapped a command into the navigation panel, and Hedwig swerved. But the set of his shoulders was stiff, and he stared resolutely ahead.

"Swift, don't be like that. Why are you—"

"Because I don't understand why you're championing this guy so much." His voice was a low hiss that only Lissa could hear. "Interlopers like him have always come to the Wildwood, and you've never shown any interest in helping them out before. What is it about this guy?"

"Nothing! I'm not— The sooner we get him out of here, the sooner he's gone, right?" A lame answer, but the best one she had at the moment. She didn't understand herself why she was trying to make Artem's life any easier.

Unconvinced, Swift simply shook his head.

They traveled the rest of the way with only the creaking of the house and the rustling of waking life as conversation. As they neared the doorway, Swift brought Hedwig to a halt. "I'm not going any further. I don't want to get blamed when this all goes wrong. Just point him in the direction of the door and let's get going."

"But there's still enough distance between here

and there for something to happen to him."

"Take him yourself then." And Swift turned away.

So she did, despite Swift's misgivings and her own unease worrying at the back of her mind. If something happened—

"Thanks." Artem's teeth flashed even in the oncoming gloom. "I'm sorry I've been such trouble."

"No, it's fine." Even though it wasn't.

The minutes stretched awkwardly between them as they walked. Normally, Lissa would've tried to make small talk, but she had no idea what to say to him. What could she possibly say that would interest someone as worldly as him? And, if his silence was any indication, he agreed.

Finally, they came close enough that Lissa figured her duty was done. He could make his way through the tunnel on his own. "Here we are." Was that it? Should she just turn and go? *Of course you should. What are you waiting for?*

He nodded and shifted uncomfortably. "Thanks. Look, I'd, uh, call you or something, but I know there's no comm service out here." He gave a superficial laugh.

There was no regret in his voice, no trace of sincerity, and yet to her horror, Lissa heard herself say, "Actually, there is. It's just on a different wavelength. If you give me your transcomm, I can program it in for you." As though watching herself from far away, she saw a hand that was definitely hers reach out, waiting for him.

At first, he didn't seem to know what to do. He gave another short laugh, as though she'd made a joke. But when she kept her hand extended, his smile fell just long enough for her to know the truth. And yet, her hand refused to drop, refused to leave her with any dignity.

He recovered first, fumbling in his pocket for his device. "Yeah, of course, that would be great. Thanks—"

"Lissa." She snatched the comm from his hand and turned away so she wouldn't have to see the amused expression on his face anymore. It took her less than a minute to reprogram his comm, but it felt like years as he stood there, watching her. At last she finished and thrust the device back at him. "Here."

He glanced down at it, hesitating.

What? Why was he looking at it like that?

Her hands. She'd been so caught up in being mortified at herself that she'd completely forgotten her hands, and now he was staring at his comm as though he expected it to be covered in slime. Horror at her own forgetfulness, anger at him for his ignorance, and even more at herself for caring, overwhelmed her. She pointed wordlessly at the tunnel that served as the doorway, threw the comm at his feet, and fled—away from his astonished face, past Swift's house, and into the embrace of the Wildwood.

SEVEN

Artem got the car to drop him off as close to the estate as he dared. After everything that had happened that day, he was in no mood to explain why he was home. He needed to unpack everything he'd seen—the monstrous plants, two-headed animals, and frog-girls. Especially frog-girls.

Lissa.

That was her name. Meeting her had been surreal. When he'd first come upon the clearing and seen her lying there on the ground, with her pale face, long red hair, and oddly simple dress, she'd looked enchanting, like a fairy tale princess. But then he'd seen her hands…and then she'd opened her eyes. He suppressed a shudder. What had happened to her? Something, obviously, because those eyes and that webbing between her fingers was not natural, not *normal*. She even had markings on her upper back and neck, just like a frog's. No wonder she hid out in the Wildwood. And to think, *she'd* stared at him with contempt like *he* was the freak. He was used to it from the people of Foxwept, given who his father was, but from a backwoods frog-girl? It was a new low.

And yet, when he threw himself down on his bed and closed his eyes, it wasn't her hands or strange pupils he saw, but her smile, her obvious mortification at her own boldness as she'd asked for his transcomm. It was kind of endearing. None of the other girls he knew would've acted like that. They would've made sure he knew exactly what was on offer for him, would've simply made demands, or been too speechless to say anything at all.

He shook his head. What a strange place the Wildwood was. He was glad to be done with it. He glanced at the wallscreen. 12:06 a.m. Should he go out? He couldn't really be bothered. At the very least, though, he should take a shower. The reek of niff-mantid was still on his chest. He wrinkled his nose. That Swift could've at least given him a shirt. But, judging from his house, he probably only had the one.

He was about to step into the steaming shower when a voice boomed behind him.

"Home already? Though I can't say I'm surprised. You were actually out longer than I thought you'd be. Which bar was it this time? The Red Dove?" His father was dressed all in black but for a red rose in his lapel. Contained within its petals was a poison his father had been immunized against. If he was dressed like that, he must've been meeting with the heads of the other firms, family organizations like theirs who operated the less savory businesses in Foxwept Province. "And you stink."

"I stink because I was out in the blasted Wildwood all day doing your bidding."

"And? I certainly hope you didn't come home just to take a shower. When I told you all not to return until you had something useful, I meant it."

So he was the first one back? *Ha! That'll burn Luka.* He'd never been better than his brother at anything, besides thinking. And thinking was considered less than desirable by his father *most* of the time. Then he caught himself. *Remember why you're doing this. It's not about winning anything more than your freedom.*

Artem shrugged, keeping his expression casual. "Oh, I found something. I just thought I should clean myself up a bit before showing it to you."

"You found something useful? On your first day?"

Artem couldn't blame Father for being skeptical. If Lissa hadn't come along, he would've still been out there, stumbling around in the dark, empty-handed, before being eaten by some over-sized beetle or something.

"Yes, sir. And I think you'll appreciate it." Under-promise and over-deliver. His father was definitely going to like what he'd brought. He'd wanted something that would make money? Artem had found it.

"Really." His father studied him for a moment, as though trying to discern if he was serious. "Fine. Bring it to my office once you've had a chance to make yourself civilized again." He turned on his heel.

"What? No 'job well done, son,' or 'I'm glad you're back safe?'" Though he wasn't surprised.

"We'll see what you brought first. Then I'll decide whether or not I'm glad you're back." And he was gone.

That went well.

Twenty minutes later, clean and dressed in clothes that didn't smell like a haunted forest, Artem opened the pack he'd taken into the Wildwood. Stuffed under everything else was his prize. He pulled it out and turned it over in his hand. A small twinge of guilt tainted his feeling of triumph, but only a little.

He hadn't intended to steal from Lissa—Swift, he didn't mind so much. Taking it had been an impulse, a decision made in a split-second. The moment he'd seen she was healed—the skin smooth and pale without even a faint scar where the injury had been—he'd clutched at that straw, his hands seeming to move almost of their own accord as soon as they'd left the room. And once he'd shoved it into his pocket, there was no going back.

He *had* to win, by any means he could—even stealing. There was too much at risk. Besides, the guy had knocked him out. They *owed* him.

His hope for freedom was fat and fleshy, a succulent that looked almost like an aloe vera leaf—except for the deep purple skin and aspic-like jelly within. It had a pleasant odor, almost like lemon. Who would've thought finding it would be that easy? It seemed almost too good to be true.

And what if it was? Lissa's tell had made him think this was what had healed her, but what if it wasn't? What if he went into Father's office in victory only to end up looking like the fool his father already thought he was?

Well, he had little choice now. Father was waiting for him.

* * *

He knocked on the heavy oak door. Tomas, the man standing guard outside, stared at him impassively, and Artem was overcome with the urge to stick his tongue out at him, though it had been years since he'd last done something so childish.

There was just something about the man's seriousness that irked him. Didn't these people realize that his father was just a man? A powerful man, yes, but still. Would it kill them to crack a smile? He scrutinized the man's face. No, probably not, but Father might. He took security very seriously. Well, his, anyway. His children's? Not so much. He could always get more.

Why didn't he call for Artem to come in? He knew he was standing there. He knew it and Artem knew it. He sighed. How long was Father going to make him wait?

Five minutes later, Artem had had enough. *Forget it. He can come to me if he wants his prize desperately enough.*

But the moment he turned, the door slid open and Father's voice rumbled from deep inside. "Where do you think you're going?"

"Nowhere, obviously." Artem crossed the threshold, shrinking into himself as he always did when he was in his father's office. The vast space was bigger than some of the houses he'd seen in Foxwept, bigger even than Loth's office, and he was the CEO of the largest medical tech company in the Blackmoth Republic. It seemed to take days to walk the path to the massive desk, made of the same oak as everything else in the room. And not just any oak, but endangered oak from the former Heartcrown region, gifted to his father for his support in some kind of civil conflict years ago. If it was something he shouldn't have, his father wanted it.

He was seized by a perverse urge to walk past all the gleaming oak, the carved busts and artifacts stolen from god-knew-where, past the bar filled with liquor bottles that cost more than the average yearly salary in Foxwept, and stand before the man that controlled his destiny, bow his head, and offer him empty hands. But it wasn't in him to give up, to surrender. If he didn't see this through, he would never be free. He was going to win this time, beat his brother and sister, and claim his only chance to get as far away from his father and this life as possible.

Father didn't bother with preamble. "Well?"

"I found this." He held the leaf out on his open palm, an offering for sacrifice.

His father's lip curled as he looked down at the broken plant in his son's hand. "That?"

"Yes. I know it doesn't look like much—"

Father leaned back in his chair. "No, it doesn't. It looks like a disgusting old aloe plant you dug out of the garbage."

Artem swallowed an angry retort and counted down from three. "But it heals damaged tissue, fast. So fast you wouldn't believe it. I thought..." He trailed off as Father stood and walked to the section of his ostentatious displays that held antique weapons. Wordlessly, he lifted down a long kindjal of folded steel and walked back to his desk. "Hold out your other hand."

"My hand? What are you—"

"Hold out your hand."

Was he serious? One look at his emotionless face told Artem he was. But if that was what it took to get the upper hand, he'd do it. Artem bit the inside of his cheek and held out his hand. Even though the kindjal was razor-sharp, it was still going to hurt.

And it did. Holy hell, did it hurt. But he kept his face impassive as Father pressed the blade of the dagger into his hand just below his wrist and drew it down the length of his palm. Blood welled to the surface, quick and hot, and Father wiped the blade on a white handkerchief he pulled from his pocket. He offered the cloth to Artem, who pressed it to the wound long enough to stem the flow.

"And?" Father raised his eyebrows expectantly.

Please, please let this work. His sister would've executed it with a dramatic flourish, but Artem just wanted to get it done. He steeled the tremor in his hand and lifted the battered leaf to the wound, pressing the jelly-like inside directly onto the cut and bracing himself for the sting. But it didn't come. He frowned. *Please, no.* He'd picked up the wrong plant. How could he be so stupid?

"Move it. I want to see what happened."

"It might need a few more minutes." Why was he stalling? If it was the wrong thing, a few more minutes wasn't going to make a difference.

"Now." Always a command.

Artem peeled the leaf off and dropped it.

His father clutched his hand and Artem fought not to pull away as his skin crawled.

"Incredible." For perhaps the first time in his life, the low tone of his father's voice wasn't a warning. It was actually...impressed? Artem glanced down at his palm as Father bent to get a better look.

The wound was almost gone. A thin line still marked where it had been, but the flesh and skin had knitted together, as though held by some invisible glue. It had worked. It had actually worked.

He had to bite the inside of his cheek again not to show his relief. He'd done it. It had taken him less than a day, and he'd done it. For once, he'd been first. And this, this was the sort of result Father liked best. Yes, it was going to make him a lot of money, but it also would make him look good, like he was helping people rather than simply profiting off them. Medical technology could easily do what this plant had done, but every single person in Foxwept would be able to keep it as a houseplant, having its miracle properties on hand rather than having to go to a center for treatment. For Father's purposes, it didn't really get any better than this.

"Where did you get it?"

"What do you mean? From the Wildwood."

"I know that." Father shot Artem his usual look of disgust. Artem's success had changed nothing between them. "I mean, how did you figure it out?" His eyes narrowed. "Did someone show you?"

The truth caught in Artem's throat. There was no reason it should; Father knew as well as anyone that there were more than a few people living in the Wildwood—people he would no doubt take great joy in ejecting if his plans came to fruition. So why was he hesitating?

"I just... It was an accident. I tripped over something—"

"Of course you did."

Idiot. Why hadn't he said he was attacked? "Anyway, a couple of woodbillies came along—you know the kind, only a few teeth and their eyes pointing in different directions—and they gave it to me." He hoped Father wouldn't see through the lie. He had a top-of-the-line first aid kit in his bag, and Father probably knew it.

The withering look his father threw him was answer enough. But Artem held his face still. That was his story, and he was sticking to it.

"That the best you can do?" When Artem didn't reply, he shrugged. "In truth, I couldn't care less how you got your hands on it." He went back around his desk and took up his seat again then steepled his fingers under his chin and regarded his youngest son.

Was this it? The moment he was finally going to be proud of something Artem had done? Artem hated to spoil the moment, but better he brought it up now than have his father find out later. "The only thing is, I'm not sure others don't know about it."

"What do you mean? The people who live in the Wildwood?"

Artem blinked. That didn't matter. They were nobody. He was worried about the people who counted, who could null the commercial value of the plant before they'd manage to capitalize on it. "No, I mean people like us."

"No. We would've heard of it, something like this."

"But doesn't that seem too good to be true? I mean, the potential of the stuff in there...I'm just surprised nobody's thought of it before."

Father gave him a look that plainly said he couldn't believe he'd spawned such an idiot. "It's currently illegal to remove anything from the Wildwood."

Of course it was. And his father was only too happy to sacrifice his children. The odds of *one* of the three of them making good on his plan was good enough for him.

Still, Artem had to ask. "*How* illegal?" Foxwept didn't have the death penalty, but felons convicted of very serious crimes had a habit of disappearing. Given the risk the Wildwood posed to the rest of the country t, he imaged the penalties were severe.

"Life in prison."

"*Life?* You sent us out on a hunch, to somewhere incredibly dangerous, knowing that if we got caught with as much as a seed on us, we'd go to prison for life?"

Again the scornful look. "Of course. That's what you risk being the head of this business."

Artem couldn't even *feel* angry. The disillusionment he'd worn like a second skin since his mother's death grew another layer. Any thicker and he would suffocate. Anger would've been so much easier—at least then he would've felt alive, not this soul-crushing numbness. Still, his voice came out calm and steady. "You've got what you wanted, so I'm going to bed. I'm done." He didn't wait for a response. "You can make the announcement tomorrow."

He was halfway across the room when, a split second before his father spoke, he knew what was coming.

"No."

He stopped but didn't turn. "No what?" But he already knew. It was his father, after all.

"No, you're not done."

"I brought you what you asked for. I fulfilled my end of it."

"Yes, you did. On the first day." His meaning was clear.

"Wait. So you're going to punish me, withhold what I rightfully earned, because I did it too quickly? That's—"

"Fair, I should think. What you've brought, I agree, is a good start. But if you managed to do that in one day, imagine what you could find in a few more." He gave a brittle laugh. "What a new thing this must be for you, being a victim of your own success." He flicked through some of the files on his desk. "You can sleep here tonight, but tomorrow, you get back to the Wildwood. The position isn't yours yet."

There was no point in saying anything more. He was dismissed.

Back in his room, he sat on the edge of his bed. What now? Even if he went back, even if he *somehow* managed to find something else, would his father ever be satisfied? Or was he just going to keep sending him out, over and over, until he finally didn't come back? What was the point of winning his freedom if he couldn't survive to enjoy it?

But what other choice did he have? If he'd been closer to his brother and sister, they might've been able to come up with another solution. But they'd been raised at each other's throats, and without their mother to keep them in check...

He was on his own. And going back was just part of the problem. He'd fluked his first discovery. How was he supposed to find something when he didn't even know what he was looking for *and* survive at the same time? It was impossible. He would be eaten alive or poisoned, or—

Or maybe not.

That girl, Lissa. She'd given him her number. Surely he could convince her to help him? But how? He couldn't exactly waltz in there and explain what his father was up to, ask for their keys so he could destroy her home. No, he had to be a bit more subtle than that.

She'd seemed to like him, hadn't she? Maybe he could use that to his advantage. Flirt with her a little. His conscience pricked at him, but he pushed it away. He wouldn't go overboard, just enough to get her help. How much harm could it do? Definitely not enough to outweigh what his success would mean.

Besides, he didn't have time to come up with a better plan.

So that was that. Tonight, he would get some rest, and tomorrow it was back into the belly of the beast.

EIGHT

"How much time do we have before we need to get going?"

For the hundredth time, Lissa wished Swift would just get some kind of clock, but he preferred to live without time's constraints. Besides, they were nearly finished. For the last hour, they'd been making their way down a list, checking off ingredients and other items, and packing them up to take back to Lissa's mother.

It wouldn't take much time to deliver the supplies, thanks to Swift's nomadic house—affectionally christened Hedwig. He'd built it himself shortly after he'd come to the Wildwood, and the two of them roamed the Wildwood together, settling in a different place every night. Swift enjoyed the myths about it that had sprung up beyond the Perimeter, retold in hushed voices by the few who'd seen it—or knew someone who had.

But even with Hedwig, they were already a day late thanks to Artem, and Lissa could practically see her mother's mouth pinching in impatience.

Swift echoed her thoughts. "Your mom's going to be pissed."

"Ugh. I know. But to be fair, what choice did we have?"

Swift's only response was a non-committal, "Mm." Things between them had been a bit off since yesterday, though Lissa couldn't put her finger on why, or even if the stiffness was from her side or Swift's. Part of her wanted to bring the issue up and clear the air, while the other was worried about what he might say.

But it seemed she wouldn't have a choice.

"Do you think we'll come across anymore strays today?" The forced casualness of his question was painfully obvious.

"I hope not." Then why had her pulse quickened, the way it did every time she thought of Artem? He was only going to bring trouble; his kind always did. Besides, aside from his dimples, there was nothing likable about him. He was arrogant, flippant, disrespectful—and burned maddeningly into her memory.

His confidence among strangers. That taut, golden, skin.

And she'd practically forced her comm number on him. Could she have embarrassed herself more? Thank goodness she'd never see him again.

Swift was watching her closely. "Are you arguing with yourself again?"

"No." But the heat in her face gave her away.

"You're not...thinking about him, are you?" He kept his gaze on his hands, organizing some dried foxglove.

Was that what the weirdness between them was about? Artem? "No," she lied, "but you obviously are."

"I can't help it."

"What do you mean?" It wasn't like Swift to obsess over things, especially not random men they barely knew.

He dropped the foxglove and all pretense and turned to her. "Lissa, do you like him?"

"Like him? I barely even know him. I—"

"You know what I mean."

Are you attracted to him? In the way you're not attracted to me? It lay between them, unspoken.

Lissa had long suspected Swift had romantic feelings for her, but there'd never been any need to bring it up, to jeopardize what they had. Before today, Lissa had always been happy to leave it at that. There was no one in her life she would've rather been with, romantically or otherwise...and maybe one day she *would* think of him the way he thought of her. But that day hadn't come yet, and now they'd run out of time to keep pretending.

But she loved Swift. *I can't lie to him.* "Did I find him attractive? Yes. But—"

"Why?" Swift slammed his fist down on the table, surprising them both. "How could you possibly be attracted to him? He's an arrogant prick. Just because he's good-looking and has money—"

"It has nothing to do with that!" Not the money part, anyway. What good was money if you never went anywhere to spend it?

"Oh no?" Swift's mouth was twisted into an ugly sneer.

She'd never seen this side of him before. "Definitely not the money. And yeah, he is good-looking." *Gorgeous, in fact.* "But that's not why."

"Then why?"

"I don't know. I just—" She shrugged. "It took a lot of courage for him to come into the Wildwood by himself."

"Courage? Try arrogance."

"Swift, what's going on?" She took a deep breath. "Are you jealous?"

He dropped his head into his hands and gave a bitter laugh. "Of course I'm jealous, Lissa. Why wouldn't I be?"

"Because you and I...we're just friends."

He scrubbed his hands down his face. His skin was flushed, and there were red marks where his nails had dug in. "I know. I just...I love you so much. And it's not that I thought we'd ever... I mean, I *hoped*, but...that didn't really matter. It's just that we're always together. My entire life revolves around you. The thought of you falling for someone else and leaving me, leaving what we have, is—" He turned away.

She reached out and smoothed a knot from his silvered hair. "Swift, he's just one man. A spoiled, rich townie I'm never going to see again." She laid her head against his back. "I love you too. I always will. But we're going to love other people—"

"I won't."

"You will. You only love me as anything more than a friend because it's safe."

He stiffened. "What?"

Should've kept my mouth shut. "I just mean that, like you said, we're always together. Maybe some of your feelings for me are because I'm the only woman you ever really spend time with. I'm low-risk." That much was true. There were lots of women—and men—in the Wildwood who would've liked nothing more than to catch Swift's eye. But he'd never seemed to notice.

He turned to face her. "Is that what you really think? That I'm so pathetic I can't even tell the difference between real love and being comfortable?"

"No! Of course not. That's not what—" Her transcomm went off. She ignored it. "Swift, I didn't mean it that way—"

"And even if that were true, you say it like there's something wrong with that. Like knowing someone inside and out means that you can't also want to be with them in a romantic—" Her comm went off again, and Swift threw up his hands in exasperation. "Just answer it. It's probably your mother wondering where we are."

She flung herself on his bed and answered the call. "Mom, we're—"

"Hello? Lissa?" The voice on the other end was unfamiliar. She checked her comm log. *Unknown source.*

"Yes. Uh, who is this?"

"Oh, sorry. It's Artem. You know, from the other day. I hit you with a rock."

Artem. "I... Hi. How are you doing?" Swift's gaze burned into her from the other side of the room.

"Yeah, great. I had a shower, so I don't smell like dead bugs anymore."

"That's great." She waited. Why was he calling her? And why was her heart pounding?

He gave a self-conscious laugh. "Listen, I know this is going to sound weird, but despite everything that happened the other day, I had a really good time."

A good time? He made it sound like they'd been out on a date that had ended prematurely. Where was this going? Hope, irrational and unwanted, budded in her chest.

"Okay, I'm glad. But I—"

"I was hoping we could do it again." The request

was so smooth, with none of the nerves that were exploding in her own brain.

"Do it again?" Why did she sound so stupid? Why couldn't she say something witty? If he hadn't thought she was a bumpkin before, he definitely would now.

He laughed as though she'd said something clever. "Yes. I know this sounds crazy, but I really found the Wildwood interesting. *And* its inhabitants." He let the last bit hang between them.

Lissa rolled over so Swift couldn't see her face. "I, uh—" What was wrong with her. *Just tell him to kick rocks. Do you really want him following you around for days with that revolted look on his face?*

"So what do you think? Would you mind escorting me around the Wildwood for a few days? Show me the sights? I promise not to throw any more rocks at you."

What could she say? Part of her brain shouted a warning, that something wasn't right. His disgust at the sight of her had been excruciatingly clear. He had to be up to something.

But did he? Or was she just being precious about the fact that he'd hurt her feelings? After all, he was asking for a tour, not a date. *That* would be suspicious. Asking for her as a guide around the Wildwood? It made sense. Yesterday had obviously been his first time in the Wood, so she and Swift were probably the only people he knew. And unless he was an idiot, he knew that Swift wasn't likely to help him. But her? He probably figured she would be more accommodating, and he was right. It was convenience, nothing more. Besides, what was the big deal? Was she really going to brush him off just because he was good-looking and wealthy? Surely that would make her a hypocrite?

The thought was sobering. "Yeah, okay, if you want. Though I don't really know what you're expecting." Good, at least it didn't sound like she was falling all over herself to see him again. *Which I'm not.*

"No expectations here other than to see an interesting new place with a beautiful woman by my side."

Was he making fun of her? If she had any sense, she would hang up now and forget him. Beautiful woman. She'd seen the way he looked at her hands, at her eyes. He did *not* consider her beautiful.

Despite her seeing right through the lie, hope bloomed grudgingly inside her chest.

Still, she was cautious. "Okay, sure. I guess I could do that. Where would you like to meet?"

If Swift's gaze grew any hotter, she was going to burst into flames and burn down the entire Wildwood.

"How about at my side of that tunnel? I'd come to yours, but I'm not sure if I can find it again—I don't have the best sense of direction." He laughed in a self-deprecating way that was too polished and she almost clicked her comm off.

"Fine. What day were you thinking?"

"How about now? I'm standing on my side of the tunnel as we speak. Well, in the general area, anyway."

"*Now?*"

"Is now not a good time for you?"

No, actually it wasn't. She and Swift had to get those supplies to her mother, and then they'd planned to spend the afternoon swimming.

But then she might not see him again.

So? Why did she care?

Because he might end up coming into the Wood on his own, and get hurt, or in trouble. Or he might bring a friend, and god knows what they'd get up to then. Better to just meet him, give him his tour and send him on his way.

She almost believed it, almost accepted that it had nothing to do with the fact that, despite having every reason not to be, she was intrigued by Artem. Drawn to him and annoyed by him in equal measure.

Anyway, it would be the best way to get rid of him for good. Once his curiosity was satisfied and he'd done his bit of slumming, he'd go home and never come back. And if he *was* up to something, maybe she'd be able to find out what. It might be important.

Keep telling yourself that.

She bit her lip. "Today is fine." Hopefully, Swift would forgive her. It was just this once, after all.

"Great. I'll see you then." And he was gone.

She lay facing the wall for as long as she could, dreading what she was going to have to tell Swift. And he wasn't about to let her off either.

"Who was that?"

There was no point pretending it had been her mother. Swift would know she was lying.

She rolled off the bed and stood. "It was Artem." *No big deal.*

Swift didn't see it that way. "Artem? What does *he* want?"

She didn't look at him, fascinated by a bug crawling along the wall. "Nothing much. He wants to meet up. He's interested in looking around the Wildwood."

"When?"

"Today. Now."

"But we have to take this stuff to your mom. They're counting on us. And *we* had plans."

"I know, but…you could take the stuff yourself, couldn't you? And we can go swimming anytime. It's not like our plans were set in stone." Except they hadn't needed to be, because she'd never broken them before.

"He's up to something." It was probably true, but the way Swift said it bothered her.

She closed up the last crate. "What's that supposed to mean? He's just curious."

He narrowed his silver eyes at her. "He's not into you. You know that, right? Guys like him…they don't fall in love with girls like you."

He may as well have balled up his fist and punched her in the gut. She couldn't breathe. She turned to face him, her best friend for nearly her entire life. "Girls like me? You mean *mutants*?"

Now it was Swift's turn to reel back. "No, of course not. I meant…I meant because we live *here*, Lissa, and he's from *there*. You're from two different worlds."

"And why does that matter?"

"I don't know, it just does." He took a step toward her. "Lissa, I'm not trying to hurt you. But I just— I know you well enough to see that you're hoping for something. Something more than a guy like him is willing to give."

Her face flamed. "I'm not asking him to give me anything, Swift. I don't *want* him to. I just figured if I could satisfy his curiosity about the Wildwood, he'd leave. And you've said yourself that he's up to something. Well, maybe I can figure out what it is."

"Do you honestly believe what you're saying? Are

you really that naïve about yourself? You've admitted being attracted to him, despite what an ass he is. And he'll have no trouble exploiting that."

"And you just assume I'd let him? Because I'm just a poor, ignorant, frog-girl." Why didn't he just come out and say it?

"That's not— Okay, that is what I'm saying. And I'm sorry if that hurts you. But I would rather hurt you now than have him do it later."

How dare he pretend he was doing something noble? "You're so desperate to see the worst in him. He's done nothing to you. You just— You're just jealous, Swift. And you were right earlier—it *is* pathetic."

She stalked out of the house and didn't look back. She was shocked at her own ruthlessness. She and Swift had never spoken to each other like that, and it was all over some man she didn't even know.

What if Swift was right, and she was on her way to being humiliated? The grain of possible truth in his words had stung; she could admit that now his house was out of sight. But it wasn't that she had a crush on Artem—he *was* a total ass, just like Swift had said... And yet, she found her herself still walking toward the doorway.

I just have to go into it with my eyes open.

Decided, she finally let the butterflies in her stomach take flight.

But as she neared the tunnel, knowing that any minute he would walk through it, her resolve failed. She glanced down at her hands. She'd betrayed herself and slipped on a pair of gloves. Underneath, her fingers looked like any other young woman's, small, with slender fingers and short, rounded nails. It was the webbing between them that made her different. When she was younger, she'd thought it so beautiful, a translucent, luminous skin that almost looked like dragonfly wings. It was only as she grew older and became conscious of the whispers and stares of those outside the Wildwood—those like Artem—that her delight in what she was turned to shame.

She hadn't been born this way. Her mother had been one of the Goldhare Horizon scientists, and Lissa had spent much of her time at work with her. Which meant she'd been exposed to the same experimental substances as the Wildwood itself, though unintentionally. Though no one was sure exactly how it had happened, the compounds had triggered a mutation that had lain dormant inside her.

They'd talked about her mutation only once, when Lissa was very small. Her mother, brought to the brink by yet another stressful day, had broken down and apologized for exposing Lissa to the toxins she suspected had caused her condition.

At first, Lissa had been baffled by the apology. What was wrong with her hands? With her eyes? She'd been blissfully unaware of how different she really was, or that different was *bad*. At least her mother, when she'd realized how Lissa felt, had stopped apologizing and instead encouraged her to never feel anything but proud of who she was. Swift was the same. So why was she worrying?

She straightened her shoulders and lifted her own chin. He wanted to see the Wildwood? The Wildwood was what he would get.

NINE

This was the last time he'd go out into the Woods. The absolute *last*. If whatever he found now wasn't enough, he would simply lie down and take whatever punishment his father meted out.

Nonetheless, Artem paced on his side of the tunnel with unexpected anticipation.

What was taking her so long? Had she changed her mind? Or had she never intended to come, leaving him waiting as a rebuke for yesterday? She'd seemed so surprised when he'd called, not to mention confused and more than a little wary. He'd nearly abandoned his plan right there and then, but he'd pushed gamely on, and she'd eventually agreed.

So what was he so restless about? Was it the guilt? He *was* going there under false pretenses, but so what? It wasn't like he had a choice.

Lissa emerged from the tunnel meters away from where he stood, her copper hair wreathed in a halo of sunlight.

He had to squint to make sure it was really her. Damn. His sense of direction was even worse than he'd thought.

As soon as she saw him, she raised her hand in greeting, though her smile was stiff. Fair enough. At least she wasn't still looking at him like he was a steaming pile of boar dung.

"Hi."

"Hi." He could understand if she felt awkward—even girls of his own class got flustered around him. But what was *his* excuse? Looking at her now, all the compliments or subtle innuendos that normally fell off his tongue seemed embarrassingly childish and affected. When she turned back into the tunnel, he meekly followed, searching for something to say.

He had nothing to talk to her about. Why hadn't he realized that before? They would have nothing in common. She obviously didn't go out to the restaurants or clubs he frequented, she didn't seem that concerned with current fashions...and he knew absolutely nothing about living in any way other than the luxury he'd grown up with. He talked a big game about seeing different things and experiencing a different way of living, but he'd never done a single thing to act on it, besides squirrel money away for an escape he'd known would never happen.

He was a fraud, and if he wasn't careful, she was going to see right through him. Then he'd have no chance at finding something significant enough to secure his freedom.

His purpose renewed, he adjusted the pack on his back and pasted on his brightest smile. He jogged a few steps to catch up with her, drawing alongside. "It's good to see you."

She nodded but didn't speak until they had come out the other side, into the Wood. "So, uh, what do you want to do?"

"I'd...I don't know, really. I just want to see things." He forced his laugh to sound casual, though his newly healed palm tingled, silently rebuking him. For a moment, he had a wild desire to just be honest with her, to lead her over to the closest log, sit her down, and spill his guts to her. Tell her *everything*. Maybe she would help him.

You're joking. How uncivilized do you think she is? Do you really think you're going to tell her that, basically, you're here at the bidding of your father, who, by the way, is one of the heads of Foxwept's criminal underworld, and if it's not too much trouble, could she please hand over the means to destroy her home? You know, if it's not too inconvenient?

"Are you okay?" She was staring at him.

What? Had he been muttering to himself? He was more tired than he'd thought. He had to be more careful, or he was going to expose himself. "Yes. Sorry, I'm just a bit tired. I didn't sleep well last night. Too excited, I guess. I can't wait to see more of this place."

She nodded, although she didn't look convinced. *Hurry. Just push forward. Distract her.* He hadn't thought it was going to be this difficult.

"Okay. Well, should we just walk? I mean, unless there's something specific you'd like to see?"

Anything that could make a fortune would be great. "No, nothing I can think of. Just give me the tour."

* * *

Hours later, Artem collapsed on the ground, begging for mercy. "I...can't go...any further." The undergrowth was cool and slightly damp, thanks to the moisture of a nearby stream. "If I take another step, I'll die."

"No, but if you roll over, you might."

Artem froze. "What? What is it?"

The entire day had been like that. He would just get to the point where he felt safe enough to relax, only to be warned off something he was about to step on or that wanted to eat him. How could people live like this every day, not knowing if their next step might be their last? It was a bit melodramatic, sure, but he'd never been so tense for so long in his life. It was harrowing. And yet here she was, not even short of breath.

But why was he so surprised? This entire place was surreal, and she was just an extension of it. All day she'd shown him things he could never have imagined, things both beautiful and deadly, like the inhabitants of another world entirely or the hallucinations in some drug-induced dream. Fungus that dripped from tree branches, its fingers pale and glossy as ice. Animals whose coats were bisected down the middle, a normal shade on one side, colored by the weirdness of the wood on the other. Trees that reeked of the dead. Others that seemed to draw him in with a siren song. The tiny eyes on their red stalks he'd seen his first day followed him everywhere, bearing witness to his every move. Even things vaguely familiar—like the trunk of some monstrous coiling vine that reminded him of a pumpkin patch he'd visited as a child—caused Lissa to throw out her arm to stop him.

"Careful. You do not want to get any of that on you." She indicated a fleshy lump that looked like some kind of mushroom. Its dark red flesh was pockmarked with oozing bloody sores, crimson pus glistening despite being in shadow.

Artem recoiled, nearly stepping on her foot as he stumbled back. "What is *that*?"

"A bleeding-heart fungus. Gross, right?"

"That's an understatement." He straightened, acutely aware of her hand on his arm. Its warmth seeped through the glove into his skin, and he didn't hate it.

She obviously wasn't so sure. The moment she realized she was touching him, she snatched her hand back and put it in her pocket, her mouth pressed into a thin line. Was her lip trembling? He didn't want her to be upset, not now. He hadn't found what he was looking for yet, and if she went home...

Besides, if he were honest, he was actually enjoying himself. Her love for the Wildwood was obvious, and he'd had to remind himself why he was here more than once. It was rare he saw someone truly joyful or passionate about something. In his family, the end goal was paramount, and any pleasure at getting there was usually entwined with cruelty.

The idea that his mission itself might actually be *enjoyable* had been so startling he'd tripped over a rock and nearly fallen flat on his face. She'd laughed at him, of course, but her laughter had not an ounce of the malice he'd expected. After all, she'd made it clear early on how she felt about people like him.

"What does it do?"

She shuddered. "It's an incredibly potent narcotic."

His interest must've been all over his face, because she shook her head in warning. "I mean it. Just a few drops of that and you'll be on another planet."

"Is it addictive?"

She pulled back a bit. "I don't know. Like I said, it's incredibly potent. Nobody ever takes it on purpose. Only if they're very sick, and then it's usually to ease their passing." She exhaled heavily. "Come on. Let's keep going." She pushed past him, giving the weeping fungus a wide berth.

"I'll catch up to you." He flashed a self-conscious grin. "I need to use the little man's room."

"Okay. I'll be just up the path. *Do not* go more than a few feet away, okay? Modesty's not worth dying for." She snorted at his horrified expression. Was she joking?

He waited for her to walk out of sight then shrugged off his pack and quickly rifled through it to find his vials. After grabbing a stick from the ground, he carefully scraped some of the shiny red goo into a glass tube then capped it. There. A powerful narcotic was exactly the kind of thing his father was looking for. It didn't even matter if it was addictive or not— either way, it was bound to be a success. His conscience jabbed at him again, but he ignored it. First things first.

A rustle in the bushes made him jam the tiny cylinder into his pocket. Had Lissa come back? He held his breath then exhaled heavily when a small bird shot out of the bushes and soared away. He was still alone.

Now what? He *should* get out of here. He'd gotten what he'd come for, after all. There was no reason to stay. Collection vials weren't the only new kit he'd brought. He'd been tracking his journey since before he'd even stepped into the tunnel. He could find his way back without her help, and she was far enough up the path that she'd never see him slipping off. It would be a clean getaway, disappearing like yet another ghost of the Wildwood.

But when his pack was secured on his back again, he went to her, toward the next marvel. All around him, the colors seemed brighter, sharper, the sounds more defined, the air somehow more *alive.*

And Lissa, at the center of it all.

Maybe her eyes weren't so creepy. Peculiar, and different, yes, but was that so bad? They were vivid and arresting, kind of like the Wildwood itself, bathed in a light so rich he could almost taste it.

Careful there, Artem, or you'll be one of those people who goes into the Wildwood and never comes out.

He'd always assumed it was because they'd had some kind of horrific accident, but maybe they'd simply found themselves at home. He was starting to see the appeal himself.

"Artem?" Lissa wasn't as far ahead as he'd thought. And she was frowning.

Crap. Had she seen him taking a sample of that weird bleeding fungus? *Think of something.* "Lissa, I—" A clap of thunder overhead nearly made him jump out of his skin. Where the hell had that come from? And when had the sky gotten so dark? Thick black clouds moved with a sinister slowness over the trees, laced with flashes of electricity. "What's going on?"

She raised her voice over the mounting wind. "A storm. They happen sometimes." Her hair whipped across her face and she hurriedly tied it into a knot at the nape of her neck. "We need to find shelter. Come on."

There was no way she'd take him to the tunnel now. And if the worry on her face was accurate, he didn't dare try to sneak back on his own. It looked like he was going to be in the Wildwood a little longer. So why wasn't he more upset?

"Follow me." Lissa started jogging back the way they'd come.

"Where are we going?" The wind snatched the words from his mouth and carried them away. It didn't matter anyway. As long as they would be safe, he didn't care where they were going. *Unless it's to that Swift's house.* He did *not* care for Artem.

Whether she'd heard him or not, she answered. "We're going to try to make it to the lagoon. There are some small caves there we should be able to shelter in."

A lagoon? In the middle of the Wildwood? Huh. Shame they couldn't just convert the whole thing into a resort.

After what seemed like ages, they finally found the lagoon. By that time, the wind was so fierce it chapped Artem's lips and forced tears from the corners of his eyes, making it hard to see. Lissa was just a blurred shape in front of him, bending and bobbing as they clung to anything they could to help them move forward.

She ducked under a large twist of vines; Artem had to bend nearly double to follow her. When he straightened, the sight waiting to greet him nearly took his breath away. The only place he'd ever seen water so clear was in manmade pools. He'd been expecting some kind of muddy swimming hole, maybe a small waterfall or two, not the shimmering azure expanse before him. True, it was being churned up by the wind, the thick vegetation around it battered and bowing under the force of the oncoming storm, but still...it was incredible. He turned to say as much and found her staring at him, a broad grin on her face.

"What?" Why was she smiling at him like that?

"You look so...impressed. I mean, your jaw actually dropped."

He couldn't help but smile back. "So? It's amazing. Why wouldn't I be?"

"I just assumed you'd seen so many wonderful things that something as basic as a lagoon wouldn't make an impact."

If only she knew how little of the world I've seen.

"Well, it does." Rain began to fall, wetting his dry lips. "Where are those caves you were talking about?"

She pointed and set off, with Artem following close behind. If he had to wait out a storm in the Wildwood, at least he wouldn't have to do it alone.

The mouth of the cave was low, forcing both Lissa and Artem to duck through the entrance. Inside, the stone cavern was cold and a bit damp, but at least it got them out of the brunt of the storm. Small caves such as these surrounded the lagoon, holes, and caverns that created a labyrinthine maze beneath the water. They made great camping places, if you took care and didn't wander in too far.

She huddled in the entrance, peering out. It wasn't often that a storm caught her off-guard. Had it really come up that quickly? Or had she just been too distracted by Artem to notice?

I've got to be more careful. About everything.

She ducked back inside. Now that they were somewhere safe, having to wait it out together didn't seem completely awful. Maybe he could tell her about some of the places he'd been. She could listen, pretending—for a short time at least—that she'd been there too.

The rain changed direction with the wind, angling into the cave. If they stayed in the entrance, they were going to get soaked. So she stepped further back into the cave and sniffed the air. Animals—*big* animals—of the Wildwood often took shelter in these same caves, and the last thing they wanted was to run into one of them. She held her breath and listened intently. Nothing. But she still wasn't convinced. Between the pounding rain and the howling wind, her senses were muddled...and they wouldn't be the only ones seeking shelter from the storm.

"Come on, let's get further in. I'm freezing." Artem shivered and began heading toward the back of the cave. "I swear that rain is coming down sideways."

"Artem, don't go too far back. We don't want to get lost." *Besides, we don't know if we're alone in here. The closer we stay to the entrance, the better.*

He merely waved a dismissal and ventured further in.

"Artem, we need to—"

He had stopped and was examining something on the ground. "Is this—"

"Yeah, an old fire pit. I'm not surprised. People use these caves for camping and stuff." She pointed to a pile of wood against the wall. "See? Swift and I..." She trailed off, suddenly self-conscious. What must Swift be thinking right now? He was upset enough that she'd gone off to meet Artem, and now they were trapped in a storm together? Well, she'd have to deal with that later.

"Let's light a fire then, shall we?" Artem flashed his dimpled grin at her and began rummaging through his pack. "I should have something in here..."

"Have...have you ever lit a fire before?" She didn't want to be rude but considering he didn't even know what he was looking for, she didn't have much hope.

"No, but it can't be that hard, can it? I mean, if—

" He winced and closed his mouth.

She held up her hand. "No need to finish that thought." She stepped back and crossed her arms over her chest. "All right, genius, let's see you do it. I give you five minutes."

He smirked. "You're on."

After twenty minutes of watching him trying to get even a spark from the ridiculous-looking contraption he had in his bag, she pushed him aside. "We'll freeze to death before you get that thing— whatever it is—to work." Quickly, she gathered her tinder and thirty seconds and two lumps of pyrite later, she was blowing onto the tiny flames, coaxing them into a fire big enough to keep them both comfortably warm. "There." She rocked back on her heels, trying not to look smug.

He was too amazed to be chastened. "How did you do that?"

She shrugged. "It's easy. You just take the pyrite and—"

The walls of the cave seemed to shudder as a roar reverberated across them.

A familiar, terrible roar. They were in trouble.

"What in god's name was that?" His whisper was harsh.

"A cougar."

"A cougar? Do you mean like a giant *cat*?"

"Yes."

He swore. "How big? And how many faces?"

"*Big*. And hopefully just one."

He stared at her in horror. "Now isn't the time to make jokes. What are we going to do?"

"I wasn't joking. And— I don't know. We definitely don't want to be in here with it, but I can't tell which direction the sound came from..." She trailed off as the dim light filtering through the entrance was obliterated.

It was between them and their only way out.

Frozen, Lissa held her breath. Maybe it would see them and the fire and go away. A normal cougar would've—but the cougars of the Wildwood were anything but normal. They were one of the few predators to stalk the Wildwood day *and* night, secretive and deadly.

Artem's rigid stance mirrored her own, his face pale in the flicker of firelight.

The cougar rounded the gentle bend in the tunnel, and Lissa's legs turned to jelly. It was *huge*. She hadn't even known they came that big. Its golden coat shimmered in the firelight as its crystalline eyes locked on them. Its massive paws were silent as it padded toward them, death on four legs, beautiful and terrifying. Its mouth dropped open, tasting the air and revealing abnormally long, sharp, yellowed teeth. Dying was going to hurt.

She didn't take her eyes off it until Artem was suddenly beside her, pushing her behind him. He brandished a flaming stick, jabbing it menacingly at the large cat.

"Get out of here," he shouted, his voice surprisingly steady.

The cougar shrank back from the flames, closer to the wall and out of the ring of light. But still it kept coming.

"Artem—"

"Go!" he yelled at the cat and charged toward it, waving the fiery brand. "Go!"

What was he doing? Was he trying to get himself killed? There was no way that cougar was going to be scared by the sight of a single man running at it, not even one with a flaming stick.

Except that it was—for a few moments, anyway. It dodged away from him, twisting as it ran.

The wrong way.

Now the entrance was clear, but the cougar was between Artem and Lissa. And between Lissa and the exit. At least Artem could escape. Maybe he could find Swift, or someone else sheltering in one of the caves. "Artem, go! Get out. Get help!" Even though it would be over long before help ever got here.

He hovered at the turn, little more than a darkened silhouette with his back to the light. What was he waiting for?

I should've been more careful. I should've—

The cougar snarled and began stalking toward her, slowly, deliberately, its shoulders rolling as it lowered itself into a crouch, coiled to spring.

Artem turned the corner, out of sight.

Lissa closed her eyes. As much as she'd wanted to leave, to see the world, she was glad she would die here, in her beloved Wildwood. Maybe this was poetic justice, a savage rebuke for not being happy with her lot.

The air was split by a scream. Was it hers? The impact she was waiting for never came.

She forced her eyes open. Artem was charging the cougar again. What in god's name was he doing? Why hadn't he run?

He was yelling her name.

The cougar leaped easily out of his way then dropped to a crouch again, snarling, but staying put. It watched them with wary eyes as Artem reached Lissa and grabbed her by the hand. "Come on."

"Where?" She couldn't keep the hysterical note out of her voice. There was nowhere to go. The cougar was still between them and the way out.

"Away from that! Does it matter?" He picked up speed, pulling her along as he darted toward the dark recess at the back of the cave. A frustrated roar nipped at their heels.

"But Artem, it's not—" The next thing she knew she'd fallen flat on her face, the wind knocked out of her lungs. And Artem had vanished.

"Artem?" The darkness swallowed her whisper whole. "Are you there?" She groped blindly in front of her. Wherever Artem was, he'd taken the light with him.

Her fingers found the edge of something. Beyond that was nothing but air.

If she hadn't already been lying down, she would've collapsed. In front of her, as wide as her arms could reach, was a hole, one of the thousands of shafts that honeycombed the lagoon. There was no doubt where Artem had gone.

He'd tried to save her. *Had* saved her. The cougar hadn't followed them, likely wary of Artem and his fire. But that fire had been snuffed out.

A coldness, indistinguishable from the tunnel floor, spread through her. He'd come back. He could've run and left her, could've saved himself. But he hadn't. He'd put himself between her and that monstrous cougar not once, but twice, and now he was gone, lost in the dark heart of the Wildwood.

I never thought he had it in him.

Who would've believed the spoiled, rich young man from beyond the Perimeter would've put himself in harm's way for *her*? Not only someone he barely knew, but someone from the Wildwood—and a freakish one at that. He could've been killed by that cougar and he was smart enough to know that. And now, because he'd taken the lead in the darkness, he'd fallen down a shaft and probably broken his neck. *If* he was lucky. She shuddered. She didn't want to think about the alternatives.

He was willing to sacrifice himself for me. And I thought the worst of him, assumed he was up to no good just because of where he came from, because of things in his life he couldn't help. I was so convinced he was looking down on me this whole time...but it was me. It was all me. And now he's dead.

"Lissa?" The voice rose from the direction of the shaft, the whisper of a ghost.

Could it really be him? "Artem?" She scrambled to her hands and knees and squinted over the edge of the hole into the darkness. "Artem, is that you? You're alive?"

"I think so." His voice sounded breathless and strained. "But for how much longer, I'm not sure."

"What? What do you mean? Where are you?"

"I'm here, just inside the...whatever this is."

He sounded so close. She scrabbled frantically on the ground around the edge until she found his fingers, clinging on to the edge for dear life.

"Are you okay?" She almost wept with relief. *He's alive.*

"I don't think I can hold on much longer."

She took a deep breath. "Okay. I can pull you up. Give me your hand."

"I can't see you."

"Right, sorry." She walked her fingers over his hand until she found his wrist. "Okay, grab on." She dug her knees and other hand into the dirt floor as well as she could. Artem locked his hand with hers, their grips tight around each other's wrists.

"Ready?" His voice was stronger, as though some

of her strength was flowing into him through their hold.

"Ready." And she pulled with every bit of strength she had. His feet scuffed against the side of the shaft as he tried to find purchase, and the muscles in her arm strained and screamed for release. But she wasn't going to let go.

Her glove had other ideas. It began to slide, slipping down her arm with a speed that was both far too fast and agonizingly slow.

"Lissa! Your glove— I can't feel your fingers!" The terror in his voice bit deep. He was clutching only the leather now, and the cuff of the tight glove was halfway down her forearm.

She didn't even have time to shout his name before the demon of his own weight tore him away from her, down, down into the blackness beyond.

In the silence that remained, Lissa panted, trying to catch her breath. The edge of the shaft bit into the soft flesh of her knees, and sobbing, she sat back and drew them to her chest. She hadn't saved him. She'd let him die. She—

What was that noise? It had sounded like water breaking, like when she and Swift jackknifed off the roof of his house into the lagoon during the hottest days of summer.

Could Artem have survived?

If there was even a chance, she had to find out. She couldn't leave him for dead. She'd never be able to live with herself. Every night she would grieve, haunted by the man from beyond the Perimeter who'd put himself in danger for her and who now floated deep under the Wildwood for all eternity. *No.* She wouldn't leave either of them to that fate.

Heart pounding in her chest, Lissa scooted to the

edge of the shaft, dangling her legs down into a dark so deep she couldn't even see her own feet.

I'm coming, Artem. Wherever you are, I'll find you.

She took a deep breath, counted to three, and pushed off from the edge.

ELEVEN

As Lissa plummeted through the cool dark with her heart in her mouth, she had enough time to think. What if she'd misheard? What if the tunnel went on and on, with no bottom, leaving her to fall for the rest of time?

You'd starve to death first.

Well, that was a small comfort, at least.

But the shaft wasn't endless. After a few seconds, the air warmed, and in a sudden kaleidoscope of light, Lissa plunged feet-first into warm water, slicing through it in a haze of thick bubbles. As they cleared, she found herself surrounded by tiny lights, darting back and forth, away from her and back again. Holding her body still, she stopped moving, stopped trying to swim, and let her natural buoyancy carry her to the surface. She broke through into a dazzling display.

The ceiling of a small rock cavern arched twenty feet above her head. Nearly its whole surface was covered with bioluminescent plants, emitting a glow bright enough to light the entire cavern. In the water around her swam numerous luminescent fish, curious about the stranger suddenly in their midst. It was like swimming in a sea of stars.

But that wasn't the most beautiful thing about it.

Sitting on the nearby bank, with his back pressed to the cavern wall, was Artem. Stunned and bedraggled, but *alive*. He was staring at her in shock, more startled by her arrival than the teeming life around them. He held out a hand to help her as she swam over to him.

She reached out reflexively then snatched her hand back before he could touch it.

Her hand was bare. Both hands. She must've lost the other glove when she hit the water.

"Lissa. Give me your hand."

Hadn't he seen her naked fingers? "I— My gloves are gone."

"So? Just give me your hand." He motioned for her to grab on.

"But—" Her skin was going to touch his. Didn't he realize that?

"*Lissa*." But his voice wasn't unkind.

Finally, she held out her hand and he helped her onto the shore. For a few minutes they sat silently, side-by-side.

He spoke first. "Lissa, what are you doing here?"

"What do you mean?"

"You could've escaped. Waited out the storm. Did the cougar come after you again?"

"No. I think he figured we weren't worth the effort."

"Then why?"

Did it matter? "Because you saved me from that cougar. You protected me. I wasn't going to leave you to die."

"But you didn't know what was at the bottom, did you? You could've died."

"So could you." She shrugged. "I couldn't have lived with myself if I'd abandoned you."

He was quiet for a few moments. "Thank you, I—Thank you."

"You're welcome. And thank you, too." They grinned at each other.

Artem looked away first. "So what is this place?"

"It's part of the lagoon. The land underneath it is a network of underwater tunnels and caverns just like this one."

"It's beautiful."

"Yes."

Artem reached out and put his hand over hers.

The weight of his fingers on hers was a burden. If they were going to escape, she needed to get rid of it first. "Artem, you don't have to do that."

He frowned. "Do what?"

Did he really not understand? "Touch my hands. I know they—"

"Lissa, those hands tried to save my life." He looked at her, his face serious. "There's nothing wrong with them."

Was he making fun of her?

He took one of her hands in his, turned it over, and spread her fingers, his own tracing her palm. "It's actually quite striking." He lifted her hand so the luminescent light of the cavern shone through the delicate webbing.

"Are you not…repulsed by them?" She held her breath. Why had she asked that? Did she really want to know the answer?

He gave her an awkward grin. "I admit that in the beginning, I was— I'd never seen anything like them. And yes, I found it—"

"Careful. Don't be *too* honest." She tried to keep her tone light. She was starting to regret asking.

"Strange. But you know what another word for

strange is? Rare. *Special.*"

She pulled her hand back, laughing to cover the turmoil inside. *He touched my hands. He's not disgusted by them.* If he was lying about not hating them, he was the best liar she'd ever seen.

He rolled his neck and leaned back against the wall. "It's been pretty difficult for you, hasn't it?"

"That's an understatement. Impossible, more like. I mean, it's not so bad *inside* the Wildwood, but if I ever want to go beyond the Perimeter...forget it. You have no idea what it feels like to have people staring at you like you just climbed out from under a rock. Hating and fearing you on sight without even having had as much as a glance from you."

And the worst, she wanted to add, *are people like you.* People who had the most seemed to hate and fear the most as well. But she wasn't going to say that to him, not with this new beginning between them.

"Actually, I understand better than you think. In fact, I know exactly what you mean."

She couldn't hold back her snort of derision. What could he possibly know about how she felt?

He smiled sadly but didn't seem offended. "I'm serious. I know it seems to you like I've got everything I could want, and in a way, it's true. But none of that means much when you're feared and hated."

"You?" Was there something she was missing? She wasn't afraid of him. And hate? She'd found him obnoxious, for sure, but not much worse than that.

"Not me, exactly.... Do you know who my father is?"

"No."

"Have you ever heard of Andrei Volkov?"

"The mob boss?" *Everyone* had heard of him. He was considered one of the most ruthless and dangerous men in Foxwept, all the more so because of his numerous "legitimate" connections.

"He prefers the term businessman, but yes. And because of who my father is, people assume I'm a monster too. Everywhere I go, people walk on eggshells around me. It doesn't seem to bother my siblings much, but my mother…she hated it. Death was probably a huge relief for her." He exhaled. "My father didn't even take that day off work."

Lissa was dumbstruck. Could it really be as bad as he said? And there she was, being just as awful. And she hadn't even known who his father was. "I'm sorry."

"It's okay. I mean, I know what you thought of me when we met."

She ducked her head. If only she could go back.

He put his hand under her chin and lifted her face to his. "But I also know what I thought of you. I was horrible."

She smiled. "I guess we can be horrible together then."

He grinned. "Sounds good to me." His face, the curve of his lips, was so close to hers. The light from the glowing moss shone on them, highlighting their fullness—

He cleared his throat. "So, uh, what do we do now? Are we trapped down here forever?"

Flustered, it took Lissa a few moments to understand what he was asking. She glanced around their gorgeous prison and made a few calculations. "Possibly. Except…" She stood and waded into the water.

"Wait, where are you going?"

"Just give me five minutes." She dove in and swam around the small cavern, analyzing the changing currents against her skin. *There.* She followed one direction, counting the long seconds in her head. The water became cooler, the current stronger. More seconds ticked by, and she counted them carefully. She had to get this right, or only one of them would make it out.

Just a few seconds under a minute. Could Artem hold his breath that long? She swam back to him, treading water as she told him her plan.

"And you're sure about this? That this is the way out?"

"I'm sure. But it's going to take us nearly a minute to get there. Do you think you can hold your breath that long?"

He shrugged. "I don't know. I think so. Can you?"

"I— I don't really need to. I can take in oxygen through my skin, so..." Would this new information change things between them again? Surely it wasn't nearly as big a deal as the differences he could actually see?

"Really?"

She nodded, waiting.

"That's amazing. I mean, it really is." Again, his expression was open, his eyes guileless. "Does everyone in the Wildwood have...abilities like yours?"

"Many people, but not everyone. And I'm the only one with my particular...abilities."

He shook his head in wonder. "Incredible."

For another few minutes, they practiced, Artem holding his breath as long as possible. "It'll be close, but I think we'll make it." There was one thing that could make him move a bit faster. It wasn't much, but it might shave a few seconds off, and that could make a difference. "Artem, I think you should take your clothes off."

He stared at her. "*What?*"

Was there a problem? "Take your clothes off. It'll help you swim faster. I'll carry them for you."

"I— Okay. Turn around."

She obeyed, smothering her amusement. She'd never have pegged Artem as being shy, not in that way, at least. Behind her came the sounds of a struggle as Artem fought to peel the wet clothes from his body.

"Need any help?"

He gave a strangled laugh. "Are you actually offering?"

She turned around as he was sliding into the water, his torso—just as smooth and sleekly muscled as she remembered—slipping beneath the surface of the water. He tossed the ball of clothes at her.

"Ready." His face was tense, and she couldn't blame him. If there was any other way...

She nodded. "Let's go."

She sent a silent prayer to the Wildwood as Artem pulled as much air into his lungs as he could.

They ducked below the surface, Artem following closely on Lissa's heels. She swam as quickly as she could without leaving him behind. If he could just keep pace with her...

But he couldn't. He obviously knew how to swim, but his strokes were rough and uncertain. *Not good.* It was going to add a few seconds to their time.

They were almost there, so close that the water had begun to lighten, when Artem began to falter.

He was out of air.

He looked at her, his eyes wide.

No. Not when they'd come this far. They were close, so close.

She grabbed his hand with her free one and kicked with all her strength, for the first time in her life grateful for the webbing between her toes. They surged forward, closer and closer to the light.

They broke the surface into dazzling blue sky just as Artem went limp.

TWELVE

Lissa dragged Artem's body onto the shore and pressed her head to his chest. His ribs rose up and down, softly, but steadily. She rolled him onto his side and struck him soundly on the back until he coughed, water streaming from his mouth and nose as he gasped hungrily for air.

"We made it."

He nodded, still unable to talk.

"Take your time."

He lay on his back, breathing heavily, and she lay next to him, partly to catch her own breath and partly to avoid staring at his naked body. The storm had ended, the sun again dappling the lagoon with golden light.

After a while, Artem sat up and began struggling back into his soaked clothing. Lissa stayed where she was, giving him as much privacy as she could. When he was dressed, they sat side by side. There was an awkwardness between them now, one Lissa didn't understand.

He ran a hand through his hair. "I guess I should go home, shouldn't I? I've lost everything I had—my pack, even my shoes." But he made no move to go. For the first time since she'd met him, his cool façade was gone. He seemed like any other young man of the Wildwood, albeit with a more expensive haircut.

"Unless…"

His head shot up. "Unless?"

"I think you should come with me. There's no way you can make it to the Perimeter in bare feet, and besides, you'll probably catch a horrible cold if you don't get warm and dry. We'll get ourselves sorted, and then I'll take you back to the doorway." She bit her lip. Was it too much, too soon? The storm and the cougar hadn't managed to scare him away yet, but surely this was where he would draw the line. He'd already seen more in the last day than most people ever saw in the Wildwood.

For a moment, he didn't say anything. Was he just trying to think of a polite way to turn her down?

Well, she would make it easy for him. "You know what? You could just wrap something around them. Maybe some of these giant leaves." She waved at a large palm-looking plant. "I'm sure you've got a lot of stuff to get back to."

He shook his head then smiled. "Honestly? I can't think of another place I'd like to be right now."

* * *

Wildholde wasn't far, but they still had a chance to talk along the way.

"So, we're going to see where you live?" He sounded doubtful.

"Yes. At the camp." Was he already regretting his decision? Was he worried she would think it meant something?

"Is that going to be okay? I mean— I know those of us outside the Wildwood aren't necessarily welcome—"

"You wanted to see the Wildwood, right? Well, now you can meet her people. Sure, some of them won't like it, but so what? Besides, you need to dry off and get something warm inside you." She had as much claim on the Wildwood as any of them, and Wildholde was her home.

So why am I so nervous?

"Thanks. I have to admit, I agree with you about my chances of making it back with no shoes. Plus, it'll be nice to be dry. I don't think I'll be going swimming again for a while." He glanced at her. "Although that cavern *was* something else. I doubt anyone outside the Wildwood has ever seen anything like that."

"Well, hopefully they won't find out. The last thing we need is swarms of tourists getting themselves lost in there."

They walked in silence for a few minutes before he cleared his throat.

"Have you lived in the Wildwood your entire life?"

"Yes. But we lived here before it was the Wildwood. Then when the Horizon Disaster happened, we stayed."

"I've always wondered why anyone stayed. It seems bizarre to me that people wouldn't just move. I mean, your home and land were taken over by mutant plants and freak animals." He shuddered.

Was he thinking of the dyahare? Or her? *Stop thinking the worst of him.*

"Not everyone could just pick up and go, Artem."

"What do you mean?"

"Lots of people couldn't afford to move, for a start."

"Didn't the government help them? Give them

some kind of subsidy?"

Lissa scoffed. "The compensation was based on the value of the land *after* the disaster. So, as I'm sure you can imagine, it was a pittance. And even if they could afford to move, where would they go? What would they do? Many of the farmers here have had their land for generations. It's all they've ever known."

"But what do they *do* here?"

"The same thing they've always done. They farm, manage the land."

"Aren't they afraid of what will happen to them? It's a pretty dangerous place."

She shrugged.

"Is that any way to live though? Barely scratching out a living?"

"Few people have your wealth, Artem, so it doesn't mean as much to them. They don't struggle any more than they always did, they've just had to change *how* they struggle." Even she could hear the chill in her tone.

"Lissa, I'm sorry. I didn't mean—"

"I know." She sighed. "It's just the ignorance about us is frustrating."

They walked again in silence, though it now lay thick between them.

Eventually, Artem tried again. "So, your mother?"

"She was one of the scientists who worked for Goldhare Horizon. She was on the team that did the engineering that eventually caused all this." She gestured vaguely around her.

"Your mother caused the Wildwood?"

"Not directly, but still enough to feel responsible. Her team told Goldhare that the methods they were testing should be used as a theoretical model only, that they weren't close to being ready to be applied outside the lab. She told them how catastrophic it would be." Lissa shook her head in disgust. "She was fired."

"I'm sorry."

She dismissed his apology with a wave. "So of course, when it all went wrong, the government sought out those original scientists. Some of them refused to become involved again, but my mother felt so responsible that she stayed to find a way to stop it spreading, to see if there was some way they could destroy it and restore the land. She's still doing it, along with some of the other scientists and people who used to live and farm here."

"Is it going well?"

She shouldn't have said anything, but it felt good to talk about these things to someone who didn't live them every day. "The government's getting fed up with our lack of progress and the cost of constantly fighting the Wildwood. There are rumors of them looking to offload it on a private investor—though I can't imagine anyone would be crazy enough to buy it. We need to give them a good reason not to sell it, and we're close, but—" The path widened, and she gestured for him to join her. "We're almost there."

They crested a small rise, and Wildholde appeared before them.

The town was striking from this view, a small urban paradise surrounded by the Wood. From here they could see the main street, lined with stores and other amenities, and surrounded by row upon row of small, neat houses painted in bright colors. People bustled back and forth, just like a normal quarter of Portfade.

Artem's jaw dropped. "When you said camp, I expected—"

"Tents and campfire? Meat roasting on a spit?"

"Well, yes." At least he had the grace to look sheepish.

Lissa laughed. "Keep in mind that there were towns and cities here before the disaster, just like the rest of the Blackmoth Republic. Most of them are buried beneath the Wildwood, but some, like Wildholde, still stand. So we're not living rough. I mean, don't get me wrong, there are people who do, but that's their choice. Wildholde is open to all who live in the Wood. And we've got all the mod cons."

Would she have thought the same if she'd been in Artem's shoes? Probably. She may not have pictured tents, exactly, but even she had to admit, the modern village carved out in the middle of the Wood *was* a bit out of place.

"There's my mom." Lissa pointed at a woman in the distance, the same red hair as hers singling her out among the group of people she was speaking with. Her stomach dropped as she recognized Swift among them. What had he told Mom about Artem? Well, it couldn't be helped now. She just had to pretend that bringing a young man in from outside the Perimeter was the most normal thing in the world.

"Come on." She grabbed his hand and dragged him toward the group with a confidence she didn't feel.

Her mother glanced up when they were a few feet away. She smiled as soon as she saw Lissa, but her expression faltered when she noticed Artem by her side. As she pushed through to the other side of the group to meet them, Lissa didn't miss her subtle glance at their entwined hands. Great. Mom would have a million questions later, but hopefully she wasn't going to embarrass her now, in front of Artem and everyone they knew.

"Lissa, you're back." Mom smiled again, but it was more reserved, the smile she normally kept for government officials or other outsiders.

Lissa dropped Artem's hand and gave her mom a hug. "Yes, sorry. I've been showing Artem around the Wildwood." She stepped back and drew him forward. "Mom, this is Artem. Artem, this is my mother, Nova."

Artem nodded and stuck out his hand. "It's nice to meet you."

"You too, Artem." Mom grasped his hand. She was looking at him oddly. "Are you Artem Volkov?"

He nodded and ducked his head. "I am, but please don't hold that against me." He grinned, but a shadow still lingered on his face and his cheek stayed smooth.

"Hm. So what are you doing here, Artem?" Mom's shoulders were stiff, her chin raised. It was a look Lissa knew all too well—her mother was on her guard.

"I— I've always been curious about the Wildwood. Lissa was kind enough to give me a tour."

"I see."

Artem's transcomm suddenly went off, and Lissa could've shouted with joy. The tension was increasing by the second, and she had no idea what the problem was. Artem was staring at his comm as though it had grown a second head. "I thought there was no comm signal out here."

"There isn't. Except here in Wildholde. I told you,

all the mod cons.”

He gave Lissa a weak smile. “Excuse me.” Turning his back to them, Artem walked a few feet away and spoke quietly into his comm.

Mom turned to her. “Artem Volkov? Really, Lissa? Swift said—” She broke off as Artem returned. What *had* Swift said? Mom loved Swift, but even more than that, she was extremely protective of Lissa. *Overprotective.* Until now, it hadn’t really mattered.

“Lissa?” Artem stood at her elbow. “I’m sorry, but I’m going to have to go. That was my father. There’s something I need to take care of.”

“Right now? Artem, you’re soaking wet, and—”

“I know, I—.” He glanced between Swift and her mother. “Can we just step over here for a moment?” They walked a short distance away, Swift and Nova staring after them. Artem dropped his voice. “I’m sorry. I don’t want to leave right now. But it’s important.”

“Your father?”

A shadow passed over his face. “Yes.”

“Is everything okay?”

He pressed his lips together. “As okay as it ever is.”

Was he telling the truth? Or was the fact that her mother and Swift were trying to incinerate him with their eyes his real reason for wanting to leave? “Look, don’t let my mom—”

“It’s not your mom. Believe me, I’ve been treated much worse. By my own family, no less.” He gave a brittle laugh.

“But what about your clothes? And—”

“I’ll be fine.”

Lissa flinched at the sharpness of his tone. What

was going on?

He winced and put a hand on her arm. "I'm sorry. I didn't mean— I'd love to stay, but I can't." His face held nothing but regret. "Thank you for today…for everything."

"Like saving your life?" If she could at least get him to smile, she wouldn't feel like this was the end.

It worked. He grinned. "Hey, I saved *your* life, remember. More than once." Then he sobered. "Lissa, I—" He reached over and brushed a strand of hair off her face with the back of his hand.

She snagged his fingers with hers and pressed them to her cheek. "Will I see you again?" Surely this wasn't the last time she would see him. How could he walk away like everything that had happened between them meant nothing to him? She certainly couldn't.

His expression was pained. "Lissa, I—

"Thom's going to Portfade now, as it happens," her mother called out. "He can take Artem with him."

Artem shook himself and pulled his hand from hers. He stared at her for a long moment then, in a rush that robbed her of breath, he crushed her to his chest and whispered fiercely in her ear. "I hope so. I truly hope so. And I'm so sorry." He released her abruptly and went with Thom, not looking back once.

"I need to speak with you." There was a warning in her mother's tone.

"What? What's wrong?"

Her mother was gazing after Artem's retreating figure, her eyes narrowed. What was her problem with him?

"Is it about Artem?"

Her mother turned to her and raised an eyebrow. "Yes. I know who his father is. Do you?"

Lissa dipped her head. "Yeah, Artem told me. But honestly, he's nothing like him."

"Andrei Volkov is not a good man, Lissa."

"I know. But that doesn't mean Artem is the same."

Mom sighed. "Let's go home, shall we? We'll talk about it on the way."

Lissa couldn't contain her impatience and as soon as they were out of earshot of the others, she let loose. "If Swift said something—"

"He told me how you met." She raised an eyebrow.

With great emphasis on him hitting me with a rock, I'm sure. "Then he must've told you it was an accident."

"He did, but that's not the issue, Lissa, and you know it."

"Then what *is* the issue?" Like she had to ask.

"Why is he here? I mean, *truly*? And why is he hanging around you? I don't—"

"Think he'd ever genuinely want to even speak to me unless he had an ulterior motive?"

"No, I didn't say that. But—"

"But that's what you think. You *and* Swift." And they all knew it.

Mom shook her head. "I'm not going to talk about this anymore, Lissa. And I'm not going to ban you from seeing him, either. I know you'd only ignore me."

"Mom, he *saved* me."

"Saved you?"

So she told her mother about the storm and the cave, how he'd tried to protect her. "If he was the kind of person you and Swift think he is, wouldn't he have just left me?"

Her mother pressed her lips together. "Maybe. Or maybe he hasn't finished whatever he's doing here yet."

Tears stung the back of Lissa's eyes. Where was all this coming from? It had only been her and Mom her entire life, and they'd always been close. "Why are you so angry with me?" They were at the door of their home now.

Mom stopped with her hand on the door. She turned and her expression softened. "Oh, Lissa. I'm sorry." She pulled her in for a hug. "I'm not angry with you."

"Then what's going on?"

"I'm just— I'm worried for you."

"About what?"

"It's clear that you like this Artem. I'm worried that you're going to get hurt." Mom opened the door and stepped through, ushering Lissa in. "And it's not just who Artem's family is. There's also your...difference."

"What does that have to do with it? Artem's seen my hands. He *knows*."

The pity in her mother's eyes was infuriating. "Dallying with you here in the Wildwood is one thing, Lissa, but do you actually think anything could come of it? Do you really think he'll introduce you to his friends? His family?"

"Oh right. Of course not. Because I'm a freak."

"Lissa—"

"No. I can't believe you. You're always telling me I should be proud of who I am. But how can I, when you're clearly ashamed of me?"

"I'm not—"

"Then why would your first assumption be that Artem's here for some evil reason? Because that's the only way he could stand to be around me?" She took a deep breath, trying to regain some control.

"But, Lissa, he's—"

"What? Out of my league? Rich? Handsome? Not a mutant?" All the bitter fears she'd been holding inside came pouring out. After all, everyone else had already taken them as truth. But things could change, *were* changing. He'd saved her, held her hand. Stayed when he could've left. No. They were wrong.

"Honey, I—"

"I know, you don't want me to get hurt. But you don't seem to mind being the one to do the hurting." She tried to stop herself when she saw her mother's stunned expression, but it had already gone too far. "And maybe you'll turn out to be right. Maybe Artem is every bad thing you think of him. But even if he is—or isn't—I'll never forget this, how you and Swift finally let the truth slip after all these years. You see my mutation as a disability, as something wrong with me, despite trying to pretend otherwise." She looked her mother squarely in the eye. "Thank you so much for letting me know." And she went into her room and slammed the door.

THIRTEEN

The moment Artem shut his bedroom door behind him, he pressed his back against it and slid to the floor. It was only a matter of time before his father realized he was home again, and Artem needed that time to get his mind straight.

How had any of this happened? When he'd first been sent to the Wildwood, he'd done it as a mercenary, with nothing more on his mind than winning his own freedom. It had never occurred to him that there would be something—or someone—in the blighted Wood that would mean anything to him, other than a tool to use against the bedamned patriarch.

He'd never expected *her*.

And he didn't even understand it himself. Everything he could read in Swift's glare, everything in her mother's eyes when she looked at him was true. He'd never be interested in a woman like Lissa. She lacked everything he and his cadre desired. She had no wealth, no pedigree. No formal education, no worldliness beyond the Wildwood. And she wasn't conventionally beautiful. Far from it. She was a frog-girl, for goodness' sake.

And yet.

Lissa had done something for him, a stranger, that

no one in his family ever had or ever would. She'd risked her life by leaping into that shaft after him, not knowing what she would find at the bottom, only that he would be there and would need help. Had that been one of his family members…well, it likely would've been over the minute the cougar showed an interest in him. He could practically hear his father's voice as he pushed Artem toward the feral cat. "We all have to make sacrifices, son." But Lissa? She'd willingly put herself in harm's way for him.

And he for her. That surprised him almost as much. Would he have been so willing to step between a giant cat and his brother or sister? He couldn't be certain. His entire upbringing had conditioned him otherwise. Yes, family came first, but by that his father meant *him*, Andrei. He was the only family that mattered. *He'd* certainly never put his life in danger for a stranger. And yet Artem hadn't even questioned it. It had been a natural reaction, no doubt in his mind that he had to save her, give her a chance to escape, even if it was the last thing he did. And he *had* saved her.

Lissa, the woman he was betraying.

Whenever he closed his eyes, her unusual ones shone out at him from the darkness. His mind jumped to the lagoon, to the starry light of the cavern casting a luminous glow between her fingers. How had he ever thought her plain? Her beauty was unique and unconventional, true, but it was beauty nonetheless.

I want to see her again.

But how could he? Sure, he could waltz back in there now, pretend that everything was fine, but what about when the Wildwood was sold and destroyed—by his family? By *him?* She would be devastated, would hate him. But what could he do? His father was a juggernaut; Artem couldn't stop him. Even if Artem refused to play his father's game, the damage was done. When he'd said goodbye to Lissa earlier, he'd been seized by a wild desire to confess, to tell her everything.

But what difference would it make? Even on the slight chance she forgave him, his father's plans would poison anything between him and Lissa.

In trying to win his freedom, he'd trapped himself further. His only choice was to cut off all contact with Lissa., limit the damage he could do to her. But...

It can't be the end.

Yes, he hadn't known her for very long, but after what had happened between them...how could he just let something like that go? Someone like her?

He couldn't. The answer was simple, the truth of it clear. This *wasn't* going to be the end between them, not if he had anything to do about it.

If he kept on this path and claimed his victory, he could stop the Wildwood from being ruined, exploited within an inch of its life. She would be angry at his deception, but surely if he managed to make it right, she would forgive him.

Yes. The more he turned it over in his mind, the more right it felt. That was what he would do. And in the end, when it was all over, they could look closer at what lay between them, and see if they couldn't nurture it into something more.

He was decided. Although he wished with every fiber of his being it was different, he couldn't see her again, not now. It was too much of a risk—for both of them. He needed to stick with his plan, no second-guessing himself.

His transcomm buzzed, and all thoughts of Lissa vanished. Father had figured out he was back.

* * *

As usual, there was no ceremony to his return. Father couldn't even be bothered to look up.

"Well?"

Imbued with the strength of his new plan, Artem couldn't resist baiting him. "Well, what?"

His father's hand paused for a micro-second. "Don't try me, boy. I've about had enough with your useless brother and sister today."

"They're back?"

"Yes."

"And?"

Now Father raised his head. "Well, that depends on you." He leaned back in his chair and gave Artem his full attention. "What have you found?"

Artem was tempted to lie, to tell him he'd found nothing. That the Wildwood wasn't worth pursuing. But it had already gone too far. Guilt twisted in his stomach, rising as bile in the back of his throat. But still, he held out his hand, the vial of bleeding-heart sap heavy in it. Miraculously, it had survived his misadventure in the lagoon.

His father eyed it with distaste. "What is *that*? It looks like blood."

"It's sap. From something called a Bleeding Heart. It's a narcotic."

"Oh?" Father's eyes brightened as he leaned forward with interest. "How addictive?"

"Nobody really knows. The people in the Wildwood avoid it because of its strength. But it's a hallucinogenic and a stimulant, according to—"

"To?"

"My source."

Father's mouth twisted into the condescending grin that infuriated Artem. He should've just put the sap into his father's coffee and kicked back to watch the show. "Yes. Tell me about your 'source.' You've been rather cagey about the whole thing." Like Artem had suspected, his father hadn't bought the whole "two passersby" story. *You were an idiot to think he would.*

"Does it matter?"

Father cocked his head. "It seems to matter to *you*. Which means maybe it *should* matter to me. Why be so vague about it without reason?"

"I thought we were trying to keep this quiet. When it's all over, and if you still give a crap, I'll tell you."

Father scrutinized him for a moment then waved his hand dismissively. "Fine. I really don't care."

He didn't? That was a new one. Usually, he had to know everything. Still, if his father was willing to let it go, who was he to argue?

Father turned the vial over in his hands. "When are you going back?"

"Going back? But I— I've already brought you two things."

"Yes, well your brother and sister are proving to be even more incompetent than I'd expected."

"So? That's on them."

"Wrong. As a family, it's on us."

Family? Now he wants us to be a family? He doesn't even know the meaning of the word.

Artem couldn't go back. How could he, after she'd saved him? How could he return and betray her all over again?

"No."

His father blinked, as though he hadn't heard him properly. "No?"

"No."

"And why not? What aren't you telling me?"

Artem's mind raced. He certainly couldn't tell Father about Lissa. It was too risky. Not only would it give his father leverage over him, but if he found out his son was dallying with a frog-girl...there was no way he'd hand leadership over to him. He knew Father's spite all too well.

"I don't want my source getting suspicious. They're not idiots, you know. Do you think you're the first person to try to make a quick buck off them?" When his father seemed to be listening, he continued. "I have their trust at the moment. But if I keep showing up out of the blue, asking too many questions then disappearing, they'll be on to me. And then I won't be able to find out anything." He held his breath. *Please, just let him accept that.*

Father stared at him, considering him with a small smile that chilled the base of Artem's spine. He'd seen that look on his father's face before, usually right before someone disappeared or had an accident. *Does he suspect me?*

But Father shrugged and leaned back. "Fine. That's fair enough. I think we've got enough for a start anyway. After the purchase goes through, we can find more products at our leisure."

That was it? He was just going to let that go as well? *Don't look a gift horse in the mouth, you idiot. Just get out now, while you still can.* He was turning to go when Father spoke again.

"Wait."

I knew it wasn't going to be that easy. "Yes?"

"You haven't asked what your brother and sister found."

"Nothing, I assume." He kept his face neutral.

"Not nothing. But nothing *good*. Your brother came back with some cockamamie idea for a tourist safari and your sister came back with a fiancé."

"A *fiancé?*" In just a couple of days? Maybe he'd underestimated her.

"Yes. The silly girl's solution was to find a husband to do her dirty work for her. Though I can't say I'm surprised. And to be fair, if she'd chosen better, it may've been a coup. But as it stands, he's got more money than sense and thinks the Wildwood is a waste of time. Said we should just fire-bomb the lot, as if nobody's ever thought of that before."

It was true. When the first winter hadn't destroyed the encroaching mutant jungle as predicted, the next thought was to simply burn the seething mass to the ground. Unfortunately, the risk of such a sizable area of land burning at an extreme temperature for the length of time required was too high. The amount of ash generated would partially block the sun and cause a catastrophic climate change in the entire Blackmoth Republic. Any fool knew that...except, it seemed, for Misha's future husband. But it was good news. Everything was still going Artem's way.

"So despite her being a complete waste of my time, I'm obligated to throw an engagement party for her—appearances and such, you know." He rubbed his hand over his mouth. "We're going to hold it this weekend, Saturday night. In the conservatory."

Artem didn't know what to say. His father had

never spoken to him like this before, like the adult he was, like a son he didn't despise. Part of him quailed. He'd waited so long, had tried so hard in his youth to have his father take him seriously, and now it was happening. So why didn't he feel good about it?

"Well?"

He snapped his attention back to his father. "Well, what?"

"Why are you still standing here? Go. I have work to do."

And Father was back. Still, it had been nice while it lasted. *You almost got me.* Still, as he left his father's office and returned to his suite, Artem couldn't shake off the last shreds of doubt.

FOURTEEN

Why had she ever said yes?

Oh please, just admit it. You've always been on the outside looking in. You want this—almost as much as you want to see Artem again.

And to be invited to such a large, public event?

He must think they'll accept me, if he's willing to be seen with me in front of them.

Swift and her mother had been wrong, and maybe the rejection she'd worried about for so long was baseless.

She'd been shocked when the package arrived that morning. It had been a couple of days since she'd seen or heard from Artem, and fear and doubt had begun to creep in. Had the storm, her mother, and Swift put him off coming to the Wildwood again? Had something happened to him? Then came a knock at the door, and with it a large, white box tied with gilded ribbon and a golden envelope with her name written neatly across it.

Confused, she'd opened the envelope first. It held an invitation, engraved on a paper-thin sheet of cobalt-blue metal, requesting her presence as Artem's guest at the engagement party of his sister. *Tonight.* A driver would pick her up outside the doorway and deliver her to him.

She hadn't known whether to throw up or be thrilled.

Her fingers had trembled so hard, it had taken her minutes to get into the box. Inside was a dress, matching shoes, and a small oblong package with a note attached. *Don't open until we're together.* Odd. Why wouldn't he just give it to her when they were together then?

But it seemed it was true; he was inviting her. He'd sent her everything she needed. Surely she couldn't actually go, though, could she? Was that why he hadn't called? Because he was sure she'd say no?

You can just send everything back. There are a million excuses you could make why you can't go.

But she wanted to. For so long she'd stood on the outside looking in, refusing to step over the line. She'd always been so afraid of how people would react to her. But now...*he* had asked her to be there. He *wanted* her to be. He'd put himself out there, trusting she would do the same.

After an hour of arguing with herself, it had been settled. She was going.

A soft knock sounded at the door. Mom. They'd barely spoken to each other the last few days, walking on eggshells. Lissa wasn't used to being at odds with her mother, and she hated it. She'd tried so hard to give her the benefit of the doubt, to see things from her point of view, but she couldn't forget the hurtful things she'd said.

"Come in."

Her mother pushed open the door. Her hands were loaded with brushes, pins, curlers...and a handful of things Lissa had never seen before.

"What's all that?"

Mom gave her a shy smile. "I thought that since it's an engagement party, I could help you do your hair."

A dam broke. Lissa started to cry; she just couldn't help it. The brushes fell from Mom's hands as she rushed to where Lissa sat on her bed. "Oh, Lissa, don't. I'm so sorry." She gathered her into her arms and rocked her gently, something she hadn't done since Lissa was small. "I'm so, so sorry."

"Was what you said true? Is that really what you believe? That Artem's only using me?"

"Lissa, I admit I don't know what's in Artem's heart. I might be wrong about him. And I admit that my feelings toward him are colored by what I know about his father. But, Lissa—" She slipped her fingers under her daughter's chin and raised her face. "I am not ashamed of you. I never have been. I know what I said upset you, and for that I'm sorry. I just can't bear the thought of you being hurt. These people…some of them will be willing to change their minds, to accept your difference, but most won't. I just need you to understand that."

"I do." And she did, all too well. She took a hiccupping breath. Now that she and her mother were speaking properly again, she could be a bit more objective about the situation.

"But, Artem invited you. So maybe I'm wrong after all." Her mother smiled, but tension still lurked beneath it.

"You still don't trust him, do you?"

Mom sighed. "No, sweetie. I want to. I would like nothing more for than you and him to have an enchanted evening together, but it seems too much like a fairy tale, doesn't it?"

"What is it about him that you don't trust?

Besides the fact that I'm a frog-girl."

"A frog *princess*," her mother corrected with a smile. It had been their joke since the taunting started, years ago. "I honestly don't know, Liss. It might be my own prejudice. Or it might be that we're so close to proving that the Wildwood is— Well, it's probably me being paranoid. But never think it had anything to do with being ashamed of you. I just want to protect you."

"I know." Lissa squeezed her mother tightly then pulled away, wiping the tears from her eyes with the heels of her hands. She was wrung out and exhausted and the night hadn't even begun. "Do you think I'm crazy for going to this party?"

Her mother sighed. "Yes. But I'm also incredibly proud of you. It takes a lot of courage to put yourself out there, and I admire that about you—I always have."

They smiled at each other, and Lissa's heart beat a little easier. Tonight was a big deal, and she needed all the support she could get.

"Lissa?" The tone of her mother's voice told her she was about to broach a delicate subject. "I— What are you planning to wear?"

Lissa laughed. That, at least, she could be confident about. She pointed to a large box on her bed. "Artem sent something."

"He sent you a dress?" A shadow crossed her face. "What does it look like?"

"See for yourself." She held her breath as her mother removed the lid and reached inside. She carefully lifted out a mass of fabric.

She gasped. "Lissa, it's beautiful."

In fact, Lissa had never imagined a dress so lovely. It was the green of the leafy canopy of the Wildwood just as the sun crested the horizon. The voluminous floor-length skirts were overlaid by a sheer fabric sewn all over with tiny, delicate leaves and minute golden flower buds. The cut of the sleeveless bodice was daring, the sheer, plunging V overlaid with the same embroidery as the skirts. The tailored waist was finished with a slim satin ribbon and bow in the same shade of vibrant green.

"I know. Do you think he chose it himself?"

Mom smoothed her hand over the detailed bodice. "I would think so. It's a very thoughtful choice." And yet, she didn't look any less troubled.

But Lissa couldn't worry about that now. Mothers fretted; that was just what they did. "So do you think you can do my hair to match?"

"Of course."

An hour later, Lissa was ready. Her mother had left her hair loose and flowing down the back, the sides elaborately woven and held back with delicate golden filigree. She'd added just a touch of makeup, darkening her lashes and coaxing a slight blush onto her already flushed cheeks. "There." She held up a mirror. "What do you think?"

The face staring back at her was...like that of any other young woman prepared for the promise of a dazzling night. "It's perfect."

"How are you getting there? Did you want me to take you?"

"No thanks. Thomas is going to take me through the tunnel then Artem's driver will meet me on the other side." She took a deep breath. "I'm going to be okay, right?"

Her mother tucked a stray strand of hair behind her ear. "Yes. Be careful, Lissa, but be proud. The world is changing, and though the people at this party might not be ready for you yet, give them a taste of what's to come." She pressed her lips to her daughter's cheek and pushed her gently toward the door.

"Aren't you coming to see me off?"

Mom sat on the bed. "No, sweetie. You go ahead. Is it okay if I sit here for a bit?"

"Of course. But, Mom, are you okay?"

"Yes. I'm just— You'll understand when you're a mother. You're not a little girl anymore, Lissa, but that doesn't mean I can't sometimes pretend you still are." She shooed her out with a wave of her hand. "Go. Have fun. And if you need anything, call. I love you."

"I love you too." She shut the door behind her. Already the night was shaping up to be a strange one. She checked her comm and swore. She'd better hurry or she was going to be late.

There was a knock at the front door. Thomas, right on time. She shifted the mysterious box under her arm. It was now or never. She opened the door.

Swift stood on the other side, silver hair in a braid over his shoulder, his face half-hidden in shadow.

"Swift? What are you doing here?" Was he going to keep insisting that she meant nothing to Artem? Could he not just drop it for one night? This night in particular? "If you're going to—"

"Apologize? And ask if I can take you?" His eyes were wary. "You, uh, look beautiful."

"Thank you." She didn't know what else to say. Why did he want to take her? He'd made his feelings for her—and Artem—more than clear, and now he was offering to deliver her to the man he saw as a rival? Was it a trick? Was he planning to spirit her away into the Wildwood where Artem could never find her?

He must've read it all in the expression on her face. He reached out a hand and said simply, "We'll talk on the way."

"How are we—"

"I've left Hedwig just outside Wildholde. I think it's the safest way." He was right. The sun hadn't gone down just yet, but the Wildwood was restless these days. They could all feel it. Perhaps it was because they were so close. And then the rest of the Blackmoth Republic would— Well, she shouldn't get too far ahead of herself.

When they reached the house, Swift helped her up the steps. "Let's head on up to the balcony. We can watch the sun go down on the way." He followed her up the narrow staircase.

"Is that champagne?" On the upper balcony, Swift had set up two chairs, a bottle of effervescent liquid, and two slim glasses on the small table between them.

Swift laughed. "I thought we could go in style."

"You really are a good friend."

"I could be better." He ushered her into a chair and filled her glass. "Lissa, I'm sorry. Not about all of it, but some of it."

That made her laugh. The house shifted as it began to walk, and she held onto the railing until it had settled into its rhythm.

"I still believe what I said. I wish I felt differently, but I don't. But I said it out of jealousy, not because I was trying to protect you. And I'm sorry for that."

"Do you still feel that way about Artem? That he's using me?"

Swift took a deep swig of his drink. "No. Not exactly. I just...it's been us against the rest of

Foxwept forever. That might change soon, but for now…I just don't believe he understands how special you are. And that's what I worry about. That he sees you as some kind of exotic…well, I don't know what. I'm worried he's lived in privilege so long that he has no idea how cruel and judgmental people can be. Just because he accepts you, doesn't mean the rest of his circle will. And if they reject you…how well will he be able to bear that?" He shook his head. "I'm sorry. I'm not making things any better, am I?"

She reached out and clinked his glass. "You're not making them any worse, if that helps." She grinned at his stricken face. "Swift, it's okay. I understand what you mean." And she did. She was just so full of hope that she didn't want to think of anything beyond tonight. Maybe it was foolhardy, but she needed this. "And you might be right. And I might regret this. But I'm tired of letting my self-consciousness dictate my life." Too long had she stayed away from Portfade, from the rest of the province, because of a few stares and ignorant taunts. At the time they'd seemed like the end of the world, but now…now she had a chance to change that. And Artem was giving her that chance.

All too soon, they'd reached the doorway. She gripped the railing hard as she stepped gingerly down the stairs. There was still time to turn back.

"You'll be fine." Swift prodded her toward the door. But she couldn't go. Not just yet. "Lissa, *go*."

"I will. Just give me a minute." Surely she wasn't going to lose her nerve now? Artem would be waiting for her. *You can't let him down*.

"Would it make you feel better if I stayed here for tonight? Then if anything happens—"

"Would you?"

He smiled down at her and cupped her cheek. "Of course I will." He was still smiling and waving as she entered the doorway.

She picked her way carefully through the tunnel. As she came out the other side, the man Artem had sent to meet her was already there, holding the door to a long black car open. He was dressed in a somber dark suit, the crisp white shirt underneath buttoned all the way up to the top.

She accepted the gloved hand he held out to her, inclining her head in thanks. His grip tightened painfully as he looked her in the eye, the bones in her hand creaking under the pressure.

"Please, let go of my hand. You're hurting me." She didn't miss the burning disgust in his eyes.

"Just trying to make sure the young…lady doesn't injure herself getting into the car. It would be a shame if you had to give the party a miss."

What was going on? Why would Artem send this man to pick her up? Foreboding filled her. *Maybe this wasn't a good idea after all. You can still turn around.* But what would Artem think if she didn't show up? *No.* She would not be cowed. What would someone like Artem do in this situation? She straightened and narrowed her eyes at him. "I said, let go."

He grinned then stepped aside, offering an exaggerated bow as he ushered her into the back seat.

She slid awkwardly across the upholstery, trying not to squash her dress. The man took up the seat across from her. They spent the rest of the ride in silence, Lissa staring resolutely out the window as the lights of Portfade rushed past.

In only a few minutes, they'd reached their

destination.

She gasped; she couldn't help it. The palatial house sat at the end of a long driveway, illuminated like the golden sun just setting on the horizon. There were so many columns and balustrades, windows and cornices that her mind could barely make sense of it. It was almost painful to look at, and while beautiful—

It was kind of garish, actually. And for some reason, that made her feel better.

Just before the car pulled up outside the grand front entrance, the man typed a message into his transcomm. "I'm just letting the young master know we've arrived." Lissa could only nod. What could she say? After the car had stopped, the man got out and opened the door for her again.

Artem was just coming down the sweeping front steps, a frown marring his face. Like the other man, he wore a black suit, but the top few buttons on his white shirt were undone. His hair was slicked back, though one unruly lock had fallen in front of his eyes. At first, he didn't see her.

"Alexi? What's going on? What do you need me for? I've got a lot—" Then he saw her, and his expression changed.

To one of horror.

He approached the car, his eyes wide and his face pale. "Lissa? What are you doing here?"

The man who'd brought her scowled at her. "Have a good evening, young *lady*." He walked away, still shaking his head.

Artem was still staring at her as though she was a ghost come to haunt him in his weakest moment.

Her mind spun. What was happening? Had this all been a big mistake? Had he changed his mind?

Had he hoped she wouldn't come? "Artem?" Her voice broke.

"Lissa, I—" He ran his hand through his hair. "I don't—"

"Don't you want me here? I was surprised that you'd invited me, but I thought—" She blinked away the tears that were starting to blur her vision. "I'm sorry, I'll go. I—"

"No! No, I— Don't go. Sorry." He chuckled. "I just— It's a bit early. I, uh, thought Alexi would've shown you more of Portfade first. As I instructed him."

Was that it? Just because she was early? It didn't seem like that big a deal to her, but who knew with these upper-class types? "So it's okay that I'm here?"

"Of course. I'm thrilled you are." He took her hands in his and leaned in for a peck on the cheek. "And you look stunning."

Her cheeks warmed. "Thank you. The dress is so beautiful. Thank you for sending it to me."

"The dress? I—" His hands were shaking. "The dress, of course. I'm so glad you like it."

Why was he acting so strangely? Was he nervous about her meeting his family and friends? She raised her chin. She wasn't going to embarrass him.

"Well, uh, I guess we should go inside."

Artem pulled Lissa into the grand house, ushering her quickly down a side corridor that seemed to stretch for miles. Her mind was still reeling. Something was going on, something she didn't understand. The way that man had *looked* at her, like she was the most disgusting thing he'd ever seen. And the way Artem was acting. This night was not at all what she'd expected.

He drew her aside into a room and locked the

door behind them. He put his hands on her shoulders. "Are you okay?"

She studied his face, trying to understand. "I'm fine. Are you?"

"I— Yes, I'm fine. Just a bit overwhelmed, that's all. I hate these parties."

"We could skip it if you like. Go somewhere else."

"Lissa, I can't. If I don't show—" The anguish on his face was so marked. Were these parties really that bad?

"Artem, it will be fine." If only she felt as confident as she sounded. Thank goodness he couldn't see the anxious butterflies trying to fly away with her stomach.

"But these people...Lissa, not all of them are going to be kind. Some of them might—"

"Look at me the same way you did when you first met me?" she joked.

He didn't laugh. "Lissa, it's not—"

"Why did you invite me, then?"

He closed his eyes. "I just...I wanted to see you. Besides, you showed me your Wildwood, now you get to see mine." He grinned weakly.

"I'm glad you invited me. I—" Her voice came out huskier than she'd ever heard it. "I was hoping to see you again."

"Yeah?" He pressed his forehead to hers and smiled. "I just wish it was under more pleasant circumstances."

Could he feel her shiver? She tilted her face up to his. He didn't hesitate. He kissed her, his lips firm and searching, his fingers feather-light on her spine. His hair had fallen over the side of his face, tickling her. She brushed it out of the way and smiled against his mouth. Her first kiss. She didn't care what the circumstances were. She didn't care about anything other than the fact that right now, right here, he was kissing her, and she was so happy her heart threatened to explode in her chest. "Artem—"

He cut her off with another kiss, his hands cupping the sides of her face. He pressed her against the door, this kiss fevered and zealous, the embrace of a drowning man clinging desperately to a lifeline.

Lissa matched his passion, pouring all her hopes, desires, and fears from her mouth into his. She splayed her hand across his chest, her fingers seeming to seek the buttons of his shirt of their own accord. All she wanted was more of him, to feel his burning skin under her palm.

He drew a deep, shuddering breath and grabbed her hand. Bringing her fingers to his mouth, he kissed them and shook his head. "Lissa, I—"

The sounds of guests arriving en masse filtered through the door, impossible for them to ignore. The moment passed.

Artem's face darkened, and he pulled away. "Let's get this over with." He sounded like a man on his way to execution.

"Artem—"

He didn't seem to hear her.

Lissa's heart was pounding, her mind again tilting on its axis. One minute they'd been soaring above it all, and now it was as though they were hurtling toward the earth and she had no way to stop their fatal descent. She scrambled for something to say, something to keep a least a shred of the moment they'd just shared from disappearing altogether.

Then she saw it on a table near the door, where she'd placed it when Artem had herded her in. "Oh, I almost forgot. The box."

"Box?"

"The one you sent with the dress." She held it up to him. "This one. Shall I open it now?"

"Yes, of course." His expression was apprehensive. Was he worried she wouldn't like whatever was in it? How could she not? The dress he'd picked out was perfect.

She lifted the lid. Inside was a pair of satiny gloves, the same deep green as her dress.

Her chest was suddenly hollow. "What are these?"

He looked confused. "They're gloves."

"I know what they are. Why are you giving them to me?"

"I—" His face flushed.

"Will the other women be wearing gloves?"

"No, but—"

"So you *are* ashamed of my hands, of the way I look. Do you have some contact lenses for me as well?" The cut of the dress. Why hadn't she seen it before? The full-cut bodice would cover the markings on her back.

The crimson of his face deepened. "No, of course not, to any of it. I just thought... Look, I'm sorry—" He grabbed the glove box and threw it into a corner. "Forget them."

Forget. Like it was that easy. Mom and Swift were right. He was embarrassed by what she was, even if he'd convinced them both he wasn't. He was just like the rest of them, and she was an idiot. She should just tear the dress off right now and throw it back in his face then leave. She would demand the car take her back to the doorway, and if it wouldn't, she would walk. Swift was waiting for her on the other side.

"Did you bring me here just to humiliate me? To parade me around in front of all your bougie friends so you could have a laugh at the hideous frog-girl?"

"No! Of course not." He grabbed both her hands in his. "Please, believe me. I didn't— That's not why you're here."

"Then why?" Her lips still burned from the kiss, only now it was like corpselure venom, dissolving her piece by piece. She yanked her hands from his and wiped her mouth.

"Because I— I thought... I'm sorry." He tried to grab her hands again. "I *am* glad you're here."

He seemed to be telling the truth. Would he really have gone to so much trouble just to laugh at her? He was pretty clueless at times, but she wouldn't have pegged him as malicious. But even if it really was just a case of "seemed like a good idea at the time," what should she do now? Slink past the arriving guests in shame and scuttle back to the Wildwood? Or stay and pretend she didn't care what they all thought?

She marched to the corner and retrieved the glove box.

"Lissa, you don't have to." His expression was anguished, a mirror of the storm raging inside her ribcage.

"I know." But she pulled out the gloves, one by one, and drew them over her hands. As she tugged them up toward her elbow, the fabric bit into the webbing between her fingers, lighting her hands on fire. "Let's go."

"Lissa—"

"I said, let's go."

He gave her the ghost of a smile and offered her his arm. She took it, and they walked the long hall together, into the mouth of the lion's den.

FIFTEEN

How could his father have been so cruel? So spiteful? And how had he even known about Lissa in the first place? Because that had to be what was happening. The invitation, the dress, the gloves...but why? There could only be one reason—to threaten Artem.

It's probably even worse than that.

His mind raced, trying to decipher his father's plan. He should grab Lissa and get the hell out of there now, get her back to the Wildwood. It would be mortifying explaining to her that he hadn't actually invited her, that it must've been his father, but that would still be better than whatever was going to happen now.

But everything was moving too fast and the next thing he knew, they were heading down the corridor toward the ballroom, Lissa walking stiffly at his side, knowing exactly what the people in there were going to think of her if they discovered her secret.

Remember the way you felt when you first met her? If these people see her hands, they're going to look at her exactly the same way you did.

Her eyes were one thing—flamboyant contacts weren't unusual, though a bit inappropriate for an engagement party. The full back of the dress hid the markings on her spine and neck. But her hands...

They would see a freak, and you know it. And then they're going to look at you.

He hadn't thought he would care that much. But as they approached the heavy double doors at the end of the corridor, his palms became slick and his chest constricted like there were iron bands around it. There was too much wrong here, too much to be uneasy about.

His father's cruelty. The judgment of the people on the other side of that door.

Himself. Because, if he was truly honest, he *was* self-conscious about what she was. He wasn't ashamed of her, not exactly, but he knew what they would all think of her—the same as he once had—and he was ashamed by how much that bothered him. He wanted to tear the thought from his head and dash it on the floor, grinding it to dust under his heel. He wished he didn't care what they thought, but he did. *That* must've been what his father was planning. To shame Artem and remind him who was in control without actually being so crude to his guests as to rub her difference in their faces.

It was yet another test—this time, for both of them. Would Artem have the balls to risk exposing his scandalous companion? And would Lissa have the gall to inflict herself on polite society?

Either way, they would fail. If they didn't go through that door, they were cowards, just as his father suspected. But if they did, they would be at the mercy of everyone in the room. What would happen if someone became too interested in her, asked too many questions? How bad would it be? They were all far too dignified to do anything to her there, at the party. But afterward? His arm tightened, holding hers fast against his side. Lying to her was bad enough, but he refused to let anyone hurt her. The best thing would be to turn around and walk the other way.

But then his father would win, his upstart son put in his place. Artem couldn't let that happen. Not just for his sake, but also for Lissa's.

Looking at her now, her shoulders set and her head high, there was no question he had to do this. She was going to discover he'd lied to her one day, and this was the moment that might save him, might be his only chance to see her again after the dust of his betrayal settled. He could point to this, could remind her that despite what he'd done, how he'd lied, that right then, he'd put her above anything and everything else—his father, his pride, his standing. Surely that would prove to her that he could be redeemed.

For her, he could be anything.

"Ready?"

She nodded, and he pushed open the door into the intimately lit room, the soft buzz of conversation in the hornet's nest.

No one even glanced their way.

He had the wild urge to shout at them, to yell until every eye in the room was on them. He would make an announcement, ripping the gloves off Lissa's hands and shouting, *look at her! Look at her hands.* That was what his father wanted, wasn't it? To humiliate the woman his son dared show an interest in? To remind him how little agency he had in his own life? Artem would kiss those hands before their horrified faces then he and Lissa would twirl away onto the dancefloor with nothing else in the world mattering but them.

Instead, he gave a strangled laugh. Then Lissa

laughed too, and the tension around his chest eased a little.

Even though no one had noticed them, he pulled her to the back of the room, away from the crowd. There, at least, they could watch what was going on and entertain themselves. Besides, it was close to the buffet table.

"Do you want a drink?"

She glanced around the room and winced at the swirling crowd. "Please. I think I might need one."

Artem couldn't have agreed more. Leaving her to watch the circus, he slipped through the crowd to the bar, nodding politely to anyone who greeted him. He held up two fingers to the bartender. "Lucéat, please."

As he turned, he came face to face with a group of young men from his family's circle. They weren't his close friends, but they'd known each for years and been together at parties like these more often than he could count.

"Artem, how goes?" One of them slapped him on the back, causing some of the lucéat to slosh over the rim and onto his fingers.

"Damnit, Ilya, watch what you're doing."

Ilya laughed like Artem had made a joke. He'd clearly been taking advantage of the free bar. "Sorry, Tyoma." He was one of the few people who still insisted on using Artem's childhood nickname. He thumped Artem's shoulder with his fist and pointed to where Lissa stood, absorbed in watching the glittering throng. "Who's that?"

"A friend of mind. Never you mind about her." The last thing he wanted was to get caught up in a discussion about Lissa.

But Ilya didn't seem to hear him. "She's very

pretty, yes?"

"I—"

"But what is wrong with her eyes?"

Was it Artem's imagination, or did the room suddenly grow quieter? He waited a few beats before speaking. When he did, his voice was low and even. Unless Ilya had had more to drink than Artem thought, he would get the message. "I don't know, Ilya. What *is* wrong with her eyes?"

Ilya looked at him for a moment, confused. Then it dawned on him, and he glanced at Artem's father, who was chatting with some of his business associates. "Nothing, brother. Of course I was joking. Like I said, she is a very pretty woman." He smacked Artem playfully on the shoulder again then walked away, glancing back over his shoulder at Artem through narrowed eyes.

Was this what it was always like for her? The stares? The whispers behind their hands over something so small? He'd grown used to it about himself, but with Lissa, he saw it all again through fresh eyes. No wonder she'd gotten so defensive.

It didn't seem that small when you first met her, either. But he pushed the voice away. Yes, he'd been a bit of an idiot, but he knew better now, didn't he?

He made his way back to Lissa and handed her the lucéat. She nodded in thanks but didn't look at him, too entranced to tear her eyes away from the spectacle around her.

His sister had gone all out on trying to throw the most lavish party their father's money could buy. He hoped she'd spent as much as she could, because after tonight, she would be dead to their father, until, of course, he wanted something from her or her husband.

It *did* look as if the money had been well spent. She'd made the inside of the house just as gaudy as the outside, which was no small feat. Everything was just how his sister liked it, all shades of white and pale blues veined with silver. She probably thought it looked elegant and sophisticated; but instead, it was as cold and lifeless as she was. Even now, she stood chatting to people with a too-bright smile plastered onto her face, her tinkling laugh as unnatural as the glacial blue of her eyes.

He glanced over at Lissa.

In contrast, she stood quietly, taking it all in, inclining her head gracefully when someone greeted her in passing. She was a warm light in the cold room, more vibrant than the rest of the crowd combined. *She does look incredible.*

And that worried him. His father had obviously gone to a lot of trouble. The color was perfect on her, but the cut... Like the gloves, it hid her difference. So why bring her here to shame Artem and then cover up what she was?

Well, the joke was on him. Artem would *not* be humiliated by his father's bigotry. He grabbed her by the hand. "Dance?" He ignored the startled expression on her face and pulled her onto the dance floor. He was *not* ashamed.

Then why do you feel you have to prove it?

He turned his back on the voice with a spin that had her falling against him. As her body nestled into his, he tightened his arm around her waist and held her there.

Let them watch. Let them see how proud he was to be with her.

Lissa's hands shook in his, but as she and Artem mixed with the rest of the crowd, she relaxed, forgetting about herself, her eyes darting back and forth as she finally got a closer look at the other celebrants.

As everyone continued to ignore them, Artem loosened up as well and enjoyed watching the party through Lissa's eyes as they moved across the room. He explained in low tones who everyone was, why they were probably here, what sins they'd committed and against whom.

Some of the time, she could only shake her head in wonder. "This is just so...different than what I'm used to, than what I've ever seen, really."

He bumped his shoulder against hers. "Now you know how I feel about the Wildwood."

"It's like being on another planet."

The crowd hushed as his father rapped on a glass at the front of the room, the chime rippling through the party. He cleared his throat. "I'd like to have everyone's attention."

He waited until the last of the murmurs had died down then raised his glass in salute. "To my beautiful daughter, on her engagement."

As the crowd clapped politely, Misha attempted to look demure and failed miserably. Her fiancé, on the other hand, was gazing at her adoringly. How long before this had she had him on a string, waiting for the right time to finally deign to choose him? The poor bastard. Having to constantly satisfy not only his sister's demands but his father's mandates as well? The man had no chance.

Luka was there too, just beyond Misha. He was smiling at her, a broad, lazy smile of victory. *He thinks he's won.* But as far as Artem knew, he still hadn't come up with much. Had Father not told him—

Father spoke again, his voice carrying to every corner of the large room. "I have another announcement to make." He cast his gaze over the crowd, searching. "Where is my son, Artem?"

Me? He's not going to—

No. His father was going to announce his ascension *now*? Every cell in Artem's body went cold, until he could've passed for one of his sister's ice sculptures. This had been his plan, and Artem had walked right into it. His father was spiteful, but Artem had underestimated just *how* spiteful. He would elaborate, not just announce that Artem was stepping up. He was going to make an announcement about the Wildwood. And when he did, Lissa would find out. She would know what he'd done, that he'd betrayed her. The fact that he hadn't known her then wouldn't matter, no more than how he felt about her now. But there was nothing he could do.

The sound seemed to go out of the room. People's hands came together silently, the thunder of their applause smothered in the vacuum. Artem could barely draw a breath as he put one foot in front of the other. He never should've stayed. The minute she'd shown up at his door, he should've left with her. At least then he might've had a chance to explain himself.

He'd resigned himself to the fact that his lies would be exposed. He'd just thought it wouldn't be so soon.

And so public.

He made his way through the silence toward his father, whose smile stretched his face like the inhuman jaws of some demon ready for the sacrifice. And if that wasn't bad enough, Luka was glowering at him from the crowd, his eyes full of deadly promise. This whole time, Artem had thought he'd been so clever, had covered his tracks.

When he reached his father's side, the older man slung his arm over his son's shoulder, like they were the best of friends. His voice cut through the hush. "As many of you know, Artem here is my youngest son." Sound rushed into the room again as the crowd gave a small, good-natured cheer. "I never knew what would be in store for my son, if he would ever make something of himself." People laughed politely, as though he'd made a joke. "But, as it turns out, he's been able to find a way to make the most barren of lands fertile. Yes, thanks to my son—who will also be taking over from me as head of Paragon—we've submitted a petition to the governor to allow us to purchase the entirety of the Wildwood."

Even the most veteran members of the crowd struggled to retain their composure. One woman's voice carried over the throng, "The Wildwood? What is it you plan to do?"

Father raised his glass to the crowd and toasted them. "What all the rich do in situations like these. Get richer."

SIXTEEN

Get richer.

The echo followed Lissa as she ran blindly down the corridor. As the crowd erupted, she'd turned and dashed for the nearest exit, elbowing her way through the horde.

Where the hell was the way out?

He'd betrayed her. Her mother and Swift were right. Artem had been using her. He was a shill for his father. He'd lied to her from the very beginning.

The deception, his keen interest in the Wildwood, the gloves. She'd been so blind. How had she been so stupid to think he was different?

There. That painting. From there, she could remember the way to the front door. She hoped.

Someone was coming around the corner. She tried the door closest to her. Unlocked. She slipped inside and locked the door behind her. All she had to do now was wait for whoever it was to leave and—

"Lissa!" Artem pounded on the door. "Please, open the door."

What was she supposed to do now? He was the last person she wanted to see. "Go away, Artem. I can't talk to you right now."

"I can unlock this door, you know."

"Don't you dare."

"But, Lissa, I—"

"I need you to leave." There was one last thud on the door then his voice was closer. "I'm so sorry. I need to explain—"

"I don't want to hear it, Artem. Please."

There was a pause then, "Okay. I'll go. But—"

"*Please.*"

The sound of his footsteps faded away. When she was certain he was gone, she finally let herself breathe. But she had to get out, now. Otherwise, when the tears came, she'd fall apart inside this hideous house, with these horrible people. She had to get away, get back to the Wildwood and tell everyone what she'd heard. She glanced down.

And she was going to have to do it in a dress she now hated, a symbol of her monumental foolishness.

She unlocked the door and after it slid open, peered down the corridor in both directions. It looked clear. Now, if she remembered correctly, the front door would be off to the left. Holding her breath as she darted from corridor to corridor, she only let it go when she was within sight of the front door. Twenty feet. Fifteen. Damn, this house was ugly. Ten feet.

"Leaving so soon? What a shame." It was the man who'd picked her up at the doorway. The dark tattoo wrapped around his thick neck seemed to undulate as he glared at her.

He moved between her and the door, his arms crossed over his chest. Was he going to try to stop her from leaving? Or did he want to intimidate her, remind her just how lowly and insignificant she was to these people.

Don't look at him. Don't even acknowledge him. She tried to step around him, but he mirrored her, blocking her way; she was trapped.

She opened her mouth to speak, but he bared his gold-capped teeth at her, and she closed it again. But part of her, the part that was beaten and bloodied, roared to turn on him, to let him feel the entire force of the Wildwood.

There was no one else around, no witnesses—

"It *is* a shame, Alexi." A woman with artfully styled blue hair rounded the corner. "I was hoping to introduce myself to her before the night ended. Andrei always knows how to bring a night to a controversial conclusion." She glided up to Lissa and linked their arms together. "Hi, I'm Blue."

The roar receded. Was this unexpected ally offering her help? What she really needed was a means to get away from here, from Artem. To get out of this dress, this night, and breathe.

The woman—Blue—seemed more than happy to offer just that. "Since I'm also on my way out, shall we go together?" Blue didn't wait for an answer but swept Lissa past the seething Alexi. His hands clenched into fists at his sides, and Lissa winced. She stuck close to the woman's side until they were down the steps and safely away from the gaudy nightmare.

As her heart finally slowed to a pace fueled only by her anger at Artem and herself, she stopped, pulling her arm gently from her savior's. "Thanks for that. Did you say your name was Blue?"

The other woman grinned widely. "Yes."

"As in the Blue Fairy?"

Blue laughed. "Yes, as a matter of fact. Have we met before?" She peered at Lissa in the soft glow of the moon. "I'm sure I'd remember your hair, if nothing else."

"My *hair?* Not my eyes? Or my hands?" She

suddenly realized she was still wearing those disgusting gloves. She yanked them off and massaged the webbing between them, the sudden relief turning her knees to jelly.

Blue shrugged. "I noticed the hair first."

Just when I thought this night couldn't get more surreal. But at least this strangeness seemed benign. "No, we've never met. But Swift's told me about you."

"Ah, Swift! Yes, I know who you are now—he's told me a lot about you. Funnily enough, I'm actually on my way to give him something. Do you want to come with me?"

How was it possible that just as she'd needed help, this woman had appeared? Coincidence? Or fairy godmother?

A valet pulled up in a sleek indigo car with darkened windows. "Well, are you coming?" Blue climbed in and reclined beyond the open door, stretching out her legs as she indicated the seat beside her. Lissa didn't need to be asked twice. It was either join this strange woman or face the scowling Alexi— or worse, Artem. She slid across the seat before the other woman could change her mind.

They pulled away into the night. Blue rolled her shoulders and smiled at Lissa. "I hope you don't mind a bit of a walk to find Swift. I know it's dark, but I'm sure he won't be far."

Lissa gazed out the window at the bright lights and dark shapes rushing past. "He'll be right on the other side."

"Oh? Did he message you?"

"No. He's waiting for me."

"That works out perfectly, then, doesn't it?" Blue leaned her head back and closed her eyes.

Was she for real? How could she—as someone who was clearly familiar with the Wildwood, and friends with the people who lived there—be so calm? Didn't Volkov's announcement mean anything to her? If he was as bad as her mother said, he—and Artem—would destroy the Wildwood, exploiting it to death, with no care for the living things in it. But none of that seemed to trouble her. She closed her eyes and smiled dreamily, like they were on their way home after a lovely evening out.

Not that Lissa wanted to talk anyway. What would she even say? That the man she'd known for a week, the man she'd told some of the Wildwood's secrets to, the man she thought she might be falling in love with, had betrayed her?

This Blue would probably be surprised only that Lissa hadn't seen it coming.

Besides, there wasn't much time until they reached the doorway. Lissa gave herself those few minutes to think about Artem. If she didn't release some of that pressure now, she would explode.

How much of him had been true? Was all of it a charade? As much as she wanted to hate him completely, to write him off, she couldn't. Some of him must've been real. The lagoon, for instance. Would he really have risked his life for a ploy? Surely not. But what was the balance? Did the parts of him that were true carry more weight than those that hid the truth from her?

She might never know. And she couldn't let it matter. She couldn't take back the last week, but she could try to limit the damage.

They had to stop Artem's father from purchasing the Wildwood. Once it became his private property, he would be able to do anything he liked with it.

Even the idea made her shiver. The Wildwood held a great many secrets; Artem had barely even scratched the surface. He and his father had no idea what they were getting themselves into…but she did. If her mother wasn't ready, too bad. Exposing the Wildwood's biggest secret might be the only way to save it, the risks be damned.

They were here. The car door closed behind them as they stepped out into the mouth of the doorway. Blue waited until it had sped off before speaking. "Shall we?"

"One minute." Lissa bent and eased the heels she'd been gifted off her feet. She tossed the extravagant footwear into some nearby bushes and gratefully curled her toes into the cool earth.

Blue raised an eyebrow. "Don't you want to keep those? They looked expensive."

Lissa shook her head. "I have no use for them." She stepped into the tunnel, the hard ground comforting under her bare feet. She was almost home.

As they stole through the tunnel, Blue moved with the stealth of one accustomed to the Wildwood. She was definitely a mystery.

"How do you know Swift?"

"We've been friends forever."

"Forever? But he—" Not once, in all the time they'd known each other, had Swift mentioned her.

"Oh, he'd never tell anyone, not even his best friend. Given his…situation, he's been sworn to secrecy for both our sakes. I have many friends, but I also have lots of enemies. The less they know about my life, the better." She grinned, the white of her teeth barely visible in the gloom. "Hence why I'm running about in the dark trying to visit him."

Maybe I don't know anyone like I thought I did. "Why were you at the Volkovs' party? What's your connection to them?"

But they'd come through the tunnel and into the shadow of Swift's house, crouched exactly where he'd said it would be, its long spider's legs tucked up beneath it.

Blue winked at her. "Sorry," she said, though her smile held no apology. "Maybe next time."

Light spilled onto the ground as Swift's front door opened. "Blue? Is that you? And Lissa? Are you okay?" He came down the steps toward them.

The pressure rose in Lissa's head and heart. What would he say when she told him everything that had happened? How would he look at her then? All this time, he'd watched her make a fool of herself over a man he'd suspected from the start, had watched the woman he had feelings for being duped by the very kind of man they detested.

While here he was, true to his word. And to her.

She shook her head, and he understood. "Go up to my room, Lissa. Use anything you need."

Lissa turned to Blue. "Thank you." What else was there to say? She had a million questions, but she couldn't even begin to make sense of them right now. Climbing the stairs with heavy legs, she left Swift and Blue behind to murmur quietly between themselves.

"Pine sent you this..."

She was too exhausted to care who Pine was or what they'd sent. She rifled through Swift's closet and pulled out one of his old t-shirts. She pressed it to her face for a minute, inhaling the familiar scent, then tossed it on the bed and started to remove her dress.

It wouldn't budge. What was the infernal seal on

the back made of? No matter how she twisted and turned, she couldn't grip it well enough to open it even a fingernail's breadth. Of *course*. It was the perfect end to one of the worst nights of her life. She was about to run downstairs for a pair of shears to cut the wretched thing off when Swift spoke behind her.

"Need help?"

She bowed her head, pulling her hair out of the way, and pointed at her back. "Please."

His fingers were cool against her flushed neck and within seconds, the humid night air caressed her bare skin. She stepped away from him and sank onto his bed, her head in her hands. "Thank you."

"Of course." The mattress shifted as he sat down next to her. "Blue's gone. She told me what happened so you wouldn't have to."

Fairy godmother indeed. "Next time I see her, I'm going to kiss her."

He laughed softly. "She often has that effect on people."

"I've been such an idiot, Swift." She raised her head and looked at him. "You were right about Artem. He was using me."

The smile he gave her was sad. "Believe me, Lissa, that doesn't make me happy. I thought it would...but it doesn't."

She leaned her head on his shoulder as he slipped his arm around her. "Why did he do all this? It's bad enough he lied to me about why he was here, but why invite me to his house? Was it just to humiliate me? Could he be that cruel?"

"I can't even imagine." He sighed. "I'm not exactly objective here."

"And what do we do now? They're going to

destroy the Wildwood."

Swift tapped his finger on his chin. "My opinion? Stay here for the night, try to get some sleep. Then first thing in the morning, we go and see your mother, tell her what happened. We'll help figure out what to do next. No matter what happens, we have to do something, or the Wildwood will...well, we both know what will happen. As for Artem—" He shook his head. "I don't know, Lissa. I really don't. What do *you* want to do about him?"

Right now, she wanted to forget him. Forget he even existed and open her eyes to what was right in front of her. Swift had always been there for her. Maybe she'd been thinking about it wrong from the beginning. So what if there wasn't the spark she felt for Artem, the yearning to touch him, to memorize the way his skin felt under her fingertips, a ghost-kiss lingering on her lips when she looked at Swift?

Swift, in his ethereal, otherworldly way that was so different to the sharp brightness of Artem, cared for her. He always had. He was like a dream, while Artem was the breaking dawn. But maybe it was enough to dream. Love didn't have to be an arrow to the heart, did it? Surely it could be gentle and familiar. And safe.

"Swift." Her voice broke over his name, so instead, she reached for the braid that hung over his shoulder and freed it from its binding. She ran her fingers through it until every strand was loose, cascading over his shoulders, the luminescent silver like a shaft of moonlight.

Swift took a deep breath. "Lissa—"

She leaned over and cupped his face in her hands, the face of the man she'd loved with most of her heart since the day they'd met. Maybe most of her heart was more than enough, and she'd been too blind to see it before now. He'd loved her despite what she was, had never lied to her or betrayed her. He'd been on her side about everything.

Except this.

He pulled back. "Lissa, I don't— Are you sure about this?" He looked down at his hands in his lap. "You know how I feel. I don't want this to be just about—"

"We won't know if we don't try, Swift."

His eyes were impossibly bright. He took a shuddering breath and slid his hand up her now-bare shoulder, ran his fingers along the sensitive skin at the back of her neck. "Lissa." His voice was low. She heard the rawness in it and nearly pulled away, but it had gone too far. She kissed him, and after a moment, he kissed her back. Her dress slipped from her other shoulder as she pushed him back onto the bed. If she tried hard enough, wanted it badly enough, maybe this could work.

His lips were so different to Artem's. Whereas his had been hard, feverish, Swift's were soft, almost hesitant...and wrong. "Swift—"

"I know. I feel it too. Or not, to be honest." He pulled away from her, his brows knitted in confusion. "I don't understand. I've wanted this for so long. Wanted you here, like this. You can't believe how many times I've imagined this very moment. And now—"

"Now it's weird." They stared at each other, horror-struck. What had they done? She'd been so angry with Artem, she hadn't stopped to think about the consequences of being with Swift. Regret didn't even begin to cover it. Would they ever be able to get past this?

Tears came to Swift's eyes, and he began to laugh. Lissa was helpless not to join him. They laughed until they could barely breathe. And when they finally stopped, the world was right again.

"We should've done that years ago." Swift flopped back onto the bed, pulling her down with him.

"Do you still want to be my best friend? Now that the fantasy is gone?" She was only half-joking. It seemed too good to be true that they could simply go back to being friends. Not with the feelings he'd harbored for her for years.

Swift chuckled into her hair as he pulled the quilt around them. "Of course. More than ever."

The relief that coursed through her was almost unbearable. If she'd lost Swift...this night had already had too many ups and downs. "What am I going to do? About...everything." She yawned, exhaustion threatening to overtake her.

Swift brushed his hands over her eyes, closing them. "Right now, you'll sleep. In the morning, we'll see how the dust has settled."

SEVENTEEN

"How could you do it? How could you be so spiteful?" Artem pushed his way past his father's lackey and into his office. The last of the guests had just left, though Father had made his excuses and disappeared right after his announcement.

Father's mouth twisted and he actually had the nerve to look surprised. "Spiteful? I announced you as the new head of the company."

"You know that's not what I'm talking about. No one even cares about that. It means nothing. You're still pulling all the strings."

His father held up a hand and his voice dropped. "Careful, Artem."

"No. Did it have to be so pointlessly vicious? Why did you bring her here, announce the plan for the Wildwood?"

"Please, son. You think you're so bloody smart, but you're not." His laugh rasped against Artem's brain like a steel file. "I knew the moment you bumbled back here that you'd gotten lucky—I just didn't realize *how* lucky." His mouth twisted as though he'd tasted something foul. "It's a new low, even for you. A frog-girl." He shook his head.

He knew the whole time. "But how?" The truth hit him just as the words left his mouth. "You put a tracker on me."

"Of course I did. You think I'm going to let my three children go off on their own? I'm insulted."

But a tracker wouldn't have told Father about Lissa. "And you tagged a drone to me." Drones in the Wildwood were highly illegal and their use severely punished, but when had any of that been an obstacle for his father?

The implications hit him with all the force of the storm. "So when we were in trouble in the Wildwood, at the lagoon...you saw and did *nothing*?"

Father shrugged. "I knew you'd figure it out. And if you didn't...well, natural selection, right?"

Bile burned Artem's tongue. "You would've let me die?"

"Artem, this is getting tedious. What's your point?" His father's scowl indicated his patience was nearly at its end.

"So inviting Lissa here, the announcement...all of that was just to show the extent of your power over me? Because I— Because of one woman?"

"You're about to become the face of this company. The last thing you need to be thinking about right now is some pathetic infatuation. And with *her*, of all people. A mutant. I don't know how you can stand it. I mean, don't get me wrong, she served her purpose. But now it's time to grow up. If it's a piece you're looking for, go down to the Red Dove."

"Lissa is not—" No. He wouldn't take the bait. "So you put your entire plan at risk—"

"No one would dare undermine my bid."

"—over a woman you say is of no consequence? Then why do it? Because I have feelings for her?"

"So you admit it?"

"Yes, I do." And he meant it. He *did* care for her. In fact, even though he'd known her only a short time, he more than cared for her.

I'm falling in love with her.

Love. *I love her.*

Love had been such a foreign emotion to him that he hadn't understood it for what it was, hadn't recognized it right in front of him. He'd known he wanted to see her again, had *needed* to. He just hadn't understood the depth of it.

He'd never loved anyone before, not the way he loved her. And now, it could all just slip through his fingers, and it would be no one's fault but his.

But that didn't mean he was going to give up. He looked his father square in the eye. "I love her."

"Disgusting. She's beneath you, you know." Father crossed his arms over his chest and delivered his ultimatum. "Forget her."

"I won't."

For the first time, his father's composure slipped; irritation darkened his face and a vein over his temple pulsed. "Then I may have to rescind your title. Perhaps your older brother would like it instead."

Artem waited for the rush of anger, the spitting rage he should've felt at his father's manipulations, but again, it didn't come. Only this time, it was because he didn't care anymore. Father could do what he liked. It had been a ridiculous idea from the beginning, anyway, thinking that being head of Paragon, of the family, would lead to freedom of any kind. He'd never had a chance, victory or not.

"Luka can have it. I don't want it." He turned on his heel. He was going to find Lissa. And when he did, he was going to beg, grovel, climb a mountain…whatever it took to make things right between them.

"If you walk out that door, I'll destroy the Wildwood."

It was enough to make Artem stop, but not enough to turn him around. "Good luck. People have been trying to destroy it for years."

"Wrong. As it turns out, people have *known* how to destroy it for years."

"What?" Why would his father think that? Surely if the inhabitants of the Wildwood knew how to return the land to normal, they would. And yet, a coldness gripped the pit of his stomach. *He's telling the truth.*

His father laughed. "Your girlfriend didn't tell you?"

He knew damn well she hadn't.

"Turns out not everyone likes living rough in the middle of a mutant jungle. All it took was a bit of…encouragement and one of those wretched scientists spilled everything." He laughed again. "Money is what matters, son." He picked up a comm from his desk and pressed a button.

"*…It's a kind of virus. It stops them from being able to metabolize.*"

"*So they would basically starve to death?*"

"*Yes. Applied en masse, it would kill them too quickly for them to be able to adapt, like they have to herbicides…*"

He clicked it off.

It was true. At least, if the man in the recording was telling the truth. And why wouldn't he be? His father's "encouragement" had probably made it clear that he had a lot more to lose by *not* cooperating. But how had he…?

"Yes. I couldn't have done it without you leading me straight to them." He grinned. "I owe you thanks for that."

He knows how to destroy the Wildwood. This was far worse than his original plan.

Now what was Artem supposed to do? If he stayed, he might be able to placate his father enough to limit the damage to the Wildwood and buy some time to…what, he had no idea, but he would figure out a plan.

Then you'll never get a chance to apologize to Lissa, to help her understand and beg her forgiveness.

At least not while it still mattered.

But if he left now, he could never come back. He could explain himself to Lissa, tell her how he felt, but what would his father do? What lengths would he go to punish Artem's insolence?

As though Father could sense his indecision, he twisted the knife in deeper. "I've already got the lab synthesizing the virus. As soon as it's ready, it can be deployed at a moment's notice."

"Even *if* that's true, you wouldn't be putting a goldmine like the Wildwood at risk." Father was bluffing; he had to be. "All that potential profit, gone?"

"Keep up, Artem." His father winced, as though he couldn't believe one of his offspring could be so slow. "I make money regardless. Sure, destroying that hellish wood *would* wipe out the fortune to be had from rare species and potential medicines, but so what? Developing the land will net me a healthy profit—and no pesky patient or ethical trials to navigate." He rubbed his chin with mock gravity.

"Not to mention the satisfaction. In fact, the more I think about it, the more sense it makes to just destroy the whole thing."

The manipulative bastard. And he would do it too—would sacrifice any miracles hidden within the Wildwood to teach his son a lesson. He was right; he had nothing to lose.

But Artem did.

He could accept losing all the trappings of his current life. But losing Lissa? He'd only just met her. But her courage during the storm, the way she'd risked her own life to save his…hell, even the nerve it had taken to attend the party. There was something there, the potential for something he'd never imagined. Not for himself. True, she might never forgive him, and he couldn't blame her for that. But he wouldn't abandon her.

Even if she never forgave him, he had to warn her that his father knew the Wildwood's secret and was willing to use it. If she told him to leave after that, he would. Then he'd do everything in his power to stop his father from carrying out his catastrophic plan.

"I'm leaving. I don't want to be a part of this. Of your plan, of this family. Of you." There was no staying; Artem knew that now. It had stopped being an option the moment he realized his feeling for Lissa.

His father gave a theatrical sigh. "Okay, you think I'm a monster? That I can't compromise?" He didn't wait for a response. "Get your frog-girl on board. Whatever goods she can give us, I'll pay her for."

He was incredible. Did he really think everyone was like him? Artem turned just enough to see his father's face. The man was serious. "You don't actually think she's going to betray her home and all the people she knows for money, do you?"

Father sneered. "Of course she will. Why wouldn't she want to improve her miserable existence? If she doesn't, she's a fool. With all that money, she could find a doctor—"

Artem started walking and didn't look back, not even when his father's lucéat glass shattered against the wall.

Lissa *was* the Wildwood, and he was going to do everything in his power to save them both.

EIGHTEEN

The sun hadn't yet reached its apex when Artem burst through the doorway and into the Wildwood. He'd packed as quickly as possible, every moment expecting one of Father's cronies to try to stop him. But it was as though Father was trying to call his bluff, trying to see how far Artem would go. His wing of the house had stayed conspicuously silent, and even though Artem felt hard eyes on him as he left, no one made any move to stop him.

The ride to the doorway had passed in a blur, one silent action after the other as blood pounded in his ears. It couldn't be too late, not yet. Maybe now that Lissa had had some time to think, she'd realized that although he'd lied to her in the beginning, he was no longer the same person. Surely she would be able to see that, even through the haze of hurt and anger? He couldn't let himself think of any other outcome.

Like if she realized just what a complete ass you actually are?

He sent her a message for the hundredth time. *Lissa. I know I messed up. But I really need to talk to you. It's not just about us.* And still nothing came back. Was she getting the messages? Or was she simply ignoring him?

It didn't matter. He'd head straight to Wildholde.

Even if Lissa wasn't there, her mother would be, and Artem was just going to have to suck it up and face her.

He stopped on the other side of the doorway to catch his breath, groping in his pocket for his tracker. He'd managed to find the doorway this time, but he'd never get to the outpost on his own.

But his pocket was empty. In his hurry to leave, he'd forgotten it.

What am I supposed to do now?

If Lissa wouldn't answer his messages, he had no way of finding her. She'd escorted him everywhere, and he'd paid attention to everything but how to navigate. *Maybe* he could find the lagoon then the path they took from there. As he straightened, he became aware of tiny white eyes on him, stretching at the end of their scarlet stalks. "What are you looking at?"

"They understand, you know."

Swift stood behind him, arms crossed over his chest. He was topless, his silver hair long and loose over his shoulders. He looked ethereal, feral…of this place. Artem was painfully aware of his ignorance. He would never understand the Wildwood, never become part of it, the way Swift and Lissa were. How had he ever thought otherwise? Even if she did forgive him, if they were able to save the Wildwood, what then?

"She's not here."

"Where is she?"

"If she wanted you to know, you would."

And Swift just happened to be here, right as Artem came through the doorway? "You're here to stop me from seeing her, aren't you?"

"Why would you think that?

"It's a bit convenient, isn't it? You being here just as I came through looking for her?"

Swift shrugged. "It wasn't *that* convenient. I had a lot to do today." He pulled his hair back and tied it in a careless knot. "She makes her own choices."

"Still, you must be here to see me. Why? How did you know I was going to follow her? After...what happened." He didn't think for a minute that Lissa hadn't told her best friend in gruesome detail about the party in general, and what a horrible person Artem was in particular.

"Because it's what *I* would've done. I would've come after her too." He cocked his head. "Mind you, I wouldn't have done what you did to her in the first place."

"Look, it wasn't me who invited her to the party. It was my father. He'd been spying on me." He shook his head. *And all of them.* "He didn't approve of...where my relationship with Lissa might be heading. So he figured out the best possible way to punish me—reveal that I'd been lying to Lissa this whole time and make her think I was ashamed of what she is." It had been perfect, right down to the cursed gloves.

"And it worked, didn't it?"

He was so smug, so self-assured, and so *right* that Artem couldn't stand it. "You're really enjoying this, aren't you?"

"Enjoying what part of it? That you've betrayed not only her, but all of us? That you've put the Wildwood in danger?" He shook his head. "You don't know even half of what you've done."

"Believe me, I do. I may not know the Wildwood, but I do know my father. And that's why I'm here."

Swift stared at him for a long time then grimaced.

"I'm probably going to regret this, but come in." He gestured reluctantly for Artem to follow him.

Artem didn't need to be told twice. He trailed Swift through the Wood, ducking and stumbling until they reached Hedwig's front door. His pulse began to slow as he sat down at the small kitchen table. How to begin? His main concern had been simply making it to the Wildwood alive.

"We'll keep moving." Swift went to his control panel and coded the navigation.

"Is everything okay?" Had his father followed him?

"The Wildwood's been agitated lately. Though I can't imagine why." But the side-eye he gave Artem suggested otherwise.

Me? What would it have to do with me?

He was about to take a seat at the table when he saw it, bunched up and tossed in the corner—the dress his father had sent Lissa.

He leaned over and picked it up. Was it his imagination, or was it still warm?

She'd spent the night here. He'd already suspected that, but seeing the dress made it real.

Swift was watching him. "You're wondering, aren't you? If we slept together?"

There was no point playing dumb. "Look, I know I have no right—"

"You're right. You don't. But don't worry, we're still just friends—*best* friends."

Artem hung his head. "I don't know whether to be relieved or jealous." After all, even a friendship with Lissa might be out of the question for him now.

Swift inclined his head, eyes glittering. "Did Lissa ever tell you how we met?"

"Honestly, no. We've haven't had much time."

And Artem certainly hadn't wanted to spend it talking about Swift.

"It was about seven years ago, here in the Wildwood. She found me."

"Found you here? When you were barely more than a child?" Swift didn't look any older than twenty.

"I was never a child."

Never a child? "I don't understand."

"I'm not human, Artem. Well, not biologically. I'm a synadroid."

A sentient android. I can't believe I didn't see it. It was so obvious now—the nuances of his movements, the symmetry...everything about him. "And you ended up here? How?"

"I have no idea. I woke up here. And Lissa and her mother happened to find me and hid me. Lissa was the first person who treated me as another living thing. She knew I was different, and she didn't care. I was like a child then, and we grew up together, here in the Wildwood."

Artem was missing something. "Why are you telling me this?"

"So you understand how important Lissa is to me. And how important the Wildwood is to both of us. It's our entire lives, Artem. If the Wildwood is compromised, we will be too."

What was Swift getting at? Artem knew how important the Wildwood was to Lissa. "I appreciate that. I just want—"

"So I need to know, what are you doing here?"

Artem was confused. "I'm looking for Lissa."

"And if you find her, then what?"

"Then I apologize for...everything. And ask for her forgiveness."

Swift was nodding along in a sage way that chafed at Artem. Well, maybe the next bit would rattle that cool façade.

"And then I would tell her that my father paid off one of Nova's scientists and knows exactly how to destroy the Wildwood. And that if he doesn't get his way, he's going to do just that."

There was a savage satisfaction at the shock on Swift's face. "He's threatened to *destroy* the Wildwood? I thought he was just looking to exploit it. Use its secrets to make himself a fortune."

"He was. But now he's threatening to simply raze the whole thing to the ground to spite me. He'll still make money from developing it, so he's not really in the mood to bargain."

"What's his price?"

Artem glanced down at his hands on the table. "I need to cut ties with the Wildwood. Go back, take up his mantle, and do his bidding."

"And Lissa?"

"I refused to…give her up. So he offered to make her part of the business too."

Swift's laugh was harsh. "Seriously? How could he think she would ever be a part of what he's planning?"

Artem scrubbed his hands over his face. "He thinks everyone's like him. He can't conceive of a world where everything and everyone isn't for sale."

"So…you refused? I mean, surely you can't—"

"Of course I did! I told him I wanted nothing more to do with him or the family business."

Swift's eyes had grown even brighter, lit by his inhuman circuitry. "I'm sure he didn't like that."

That was an understatement. "I'm afraid I've made things worse. He's going to strike as soon as he can now. And I have no idea how to stop him."

"And what if Lissa doesn't forgive you? Doesn't want to have anything to do with you? Would you still care about saving the Wildwood then?"

He'd asked himself the same question, hadn't he? "Yes, I would. I care for Lissa, whether she feels the same or not." He laughed. "Maybe I'm pathetic. But Lissa is the Wildwood. And if I can do anything to save it, I will."

There was a noise on the stairs leading to the upper level, and Lissa came down them slowly, her legs bare under an over-sized shirt that skimmed the middle of her thighs.

She's here. His breath caught in his throat. How much had she—

"I heard everything."

What did she think of him now? If he'd known she was listening, would he have phrased it differently? No. The time for that had passed. He lifted his chin. From now on, he was going to be completely honest with her—and himself.

"Lissa, I—"

"I know. Like I said, I heard. And believe me, we're going to talk about it. But if what you said is true—and I believe it is—then we need to act fast."

She hadn't asked him to leave. She'd listened to him, and most importantly, she believed him. For now, it was enough. The rest they could figure out later. "What do we do?"

She glanced at Swift and nodded. "It's time to speak with my mother."

NINETEEN

As the house lumbered through the Wildwood, the awkward silence inside it was stifling. After the initial buzz of deciding on a course of action, the comparative calm of carrying it out was almost anticlimactic. Throw in the sickening fear that the Wildwood was in danger and the wonder that Artem truly had feelings for her, had disowned his entire life for her...it was almost more than she could bear. Even though she was sitting down, she clutched the edge of the table to keep herself present.

Think of something to say. Anything.

But there was nothing that wouldn't open some kind of floodgate, so Lissa stayed quiet and still, balancing on the tension like a spider walking on water.

One step at a time.

They arrived just as Lissa didn't think she could stand the strain any longer. She wanted to scream with relief as the house shuddered to a halt then gently lowered its massive body to the ground. She jumped out of the front door the moment it opened, landing hard on the bottom step.

Where was her mother? At this time of day, she would be...right there, going over some test results with Stella, one of the other scientists. They were so absorbed in their discussion that they didn't notice her. She shifted impatiently from foot to foot, trying to let them finish. But she couldn't, or she would explode.

She grabbed her mother's elbow. "Mom? I'm so sorry to interrupt, but we…we really need to talk to you."

Her mother frowned but nodded and pointed to the home she and Lissa shared.

The tension that had plagued them in Swift's house followed them there, stalking them on clumsy paws. Thankfully, they didn't have long to wait.

Mom came in minutes later, her face pinched with concern. "Is everything all right?" She glanced from Artem's disheveled state to the shirt Lissa wore, which was clearly not her own.

"No, not at all." Where should she start? "Ar—"

"My father knows how to destroy the Wildwood."

"*What?*" The color drained from her face.

Lissa leaped up and led her mother to a chair. "Mom, sit. Please."

She followed her daughter's instructions, but she wasn't going to remain seated for long.

"How?" Then it seemed to hit her, and her face grew even paler as she turned to her daughter. "You told him? *Him?* After what I said to you—"

"No, I didn't. Promise. I would never—" The doubt on her mother's face stung.

"He had me followed with an illegal drone. I led him straight here—not on purpose," Artem said hurriedly. "But once he realized what he was on to, he stopped following me and started spying on you instead. He heard everything. And that's not all." He shifted uncomfortably. "He managed to pay one of your scientists to give him the exact details—and to come and work for him."

Now her mother's face grew scarlet. "Danson, that son of a— I knew there was something up with him. I mean, the man has always sweated a lot, but the last twenty-four hours you'd have thought we were in the tropics." She exhaled heavily. "I should've guessed when he didn't show up for his shift. That man never gave up an opportunity to make money, even when he was sick."

"I'm sure my father made it worth his while."

Mom nodded slowly, as if she was only half-listening. "So what's his plan then? Sell the virus to the government?"

Artem scoffed. "You're thinking too small. His plan was to lowball the government with a purchase offer for the Wildwood, with an eye to wringing as much money from its resources as he could before destroying it for real estate and agriculture." He looked down at his hands. "Only now he's simply going to destroy it and sacrifice its resources."

Nova looked at him sharply. "What do *you* know about the Wildwood's resources?"

"I—"

"I told him." Mom was going to find out one way or another. Besides, Lissa knew exactly how she was going to react and had prepared herself for it. "Not on purpose. At the time I thought he was just interested. I—" *I wanted him to be interested.*

The disappointment on her face was textbook.

"I know, Mom, and I'm sorry. But, please, can we talk about it later?"

The quiet way her mother nodded in agreement was worse, by far. *She doesn't even seem that surprised.*

Artem jumped to her defense. "It wasn't Lissa's fault. I…made her think the situation was different than it was." He shook his head. "No, that's not right. I outright lied to her. And I used her. I wasn't trying to hurt her…but I did." He smiled sadly at her. "I can't change it, although I wish I could. All I can do now is try to fix it."

"You'd go against your father?"

"I already am, just by being here. His offer was simple. Stay there with him and he'd exploit then destroy. Come after Lissa, and it's straight to annihilation."

Her mother was looking at him now with something more than suspicion.

"Mom, I think we need to tell him." It had been the first thought that had come to her as she'd eavesdropped on Swift and Artem. It was risky, and it would mean exposing the Wildwood to the entire country, but she couldn't see another option. If they wanted to save the Wildwood, they would have to go all-in. And Artem might be the only one who could help them.

Nova glanced between them then at Swift. "I hope you know more about what's gone on these last few days, not only between my daughter and this man, but between him and the Wildwood. My gut instinct is to lose him somewhere inside it then come up with a plan. But I want to know what you think."

Her mother trusted Swift as much as she trusted Lissa. Probably more at the moment. What would he say? Swift's face was impassive, his perfect synadroid features composed.

Finally, he spoke. "I think we can trust him." A simple answer, yet one that changed everything.

"So you think we should tell him?" When he

nodded, she held up her hands in surrender. "Then I agree. Lissa? Do you want to explain it to him? I want to just check a few things with Swift if this is the path we're going to take."

Artem's gaze volleyed back and forth between them. Did he have any clue what she was about to tell him? She doubted it.

She was right.

"Lissa, what's going on?"

"Your father can't destroy the Wildwood. Or exploit it."

"I know, that's why I'm here. I'm not going to let him destroy your home—"

"It's not just about it being my home, Artem. If the Wildwood is destroyed, I would survive—everyone here would. We would have to adjust, true, but we've adjusted before. We would find a way."

"That still doesn't mean it should happen—"

"No, it *can't* happen. But not because of us."

His face was a picture of confusion. "I don't understand."

"The last few years, we've been building a plan ourselves, a way to save the Wildwood. But we were waiting until we were sure we were ready. We're still not as prepared as we'd like, but if your father is moving against the Wildwood now, we don't have a choice. We've run out of time."

"Lissa, I still don't understand. What could be more important than the people who live in the Wildwood?

"The Wildwood itself."

"But the Wildwood is—" He winced and fell silent.

"An abomination, a mutation. Unnatural." She smiled. "Believe me, I know."

"Lissa, I—"

She shook her head. "No, Artem. I get it. I know the devastation wrought by the Wildwood. But there's another way. A way that the Wildwood and the rest of Foxwept can live together."

"Which is?"

"We become a liaison between them."

"A liaison? I know it's a living thing, but, Lissa, we can't speak to the Wildwood. It would be a one-sided relationship."

"But we *can*. I mean, not fluently, but enough."

"Not fluently? What are you—"

"The Wildwood is more than alive, Artem. It's *sentient*."

TWENTY

Had he heard her right? Sentient? The Wildwood was not just alive, but truly conscious? "But *how?*"

Lissa's mother and Swift had finished their conversation. One look at Artem was all Nova needed. "You told him, then?"

"I did. But it might be easier if you explain it to him." She scooted her chair over to make room.

Nova sat. "I'll give you the short version. Basically, we suspected something was different about the Wildwood only a year or so after the dust from the disaster had settled. But it was nothing we could put our fingers on. We couldn't see it, hear it…it was just a feeling, like the air was different. And then, after studying the patterns for a while, Swift realized what it was.

"The plants were speaking to one another, communicating. They were warning each other about danger—animals, people, other pests—predicting the weather, water shortages and the like, and adapting accordingly."

They speak to each other? "But how—"

"Ultrasonics."

"You mean soundwaves?"

"Yes, but with a much higher frequency than the human ear can hear. But as a synadroid, Swift was able to pick up the waves and analyze them."

"Your middle ears are really very limited." Swift had joined them at the table.

Artem's mind leaped ahead. If this was going where he thought it was, it could work. "Does the Wood officially meet the criteria for sentience? The same way synadroids do?" Though Swift may have been secreted away in the Wildwood for the years since the Goldhare Horizon Disaster, other synadroids in Foxwept had been emancipated, their sentience recognized and upheld by law.

"Technically, yes. And if not, it's still momentous enough to force a change of legislature."

It just seemed so impossible. He didn't doubt Swift, not really, but was he the only one who could hear these plants speaking to each other? Because if he was, they had a problem. They probably wouldn't even get a foot in the door. He tried to phrase it as tactfully as he could. "Can...can anyone hear them talking but you, Swift?"

"You can. If you like."

He could? Was this some more of that mystical bullshit he seemed so fond of? *Just listen and the forest will speak to you.* He was filled with the urge to slap himself. *Now you really do sound just like your father.* "Really?"

"Of course." Lissa stood and disappeared into a back room. She returned a few seconds later with two tiny pods cupped in her palm. "Sorry. We probably should've started with that." She dropped the buds into his hand. "Here, put these in your ears." She handed a small device to Swift.

Artem did as instructed, slipping one of the nodes into each ear. At first, he could hear nothing. "I don't—"

A series of low clicks filtered through the earbuds. As Swift adjusted the device, the sounds came in to focus. The buzz of conversation filled his ears. Voices, *humanoid* voices. Chatting, laughing. He couldn't help himself; he rose from the table and made his way through the front door. There had to be a group of people standing outside.

"Artem—"

There was no one there. He walked to the edge of the Wood bordering Wildholde. How had he not noticed it before? Or had his subconscious been trying to tell him this the whole time? It seemed so obvious now that he could hear them. They leaned in, spoke to their neighbors then continued the conversation in other directions. The whole wood was alive with conversation, of lives consciously lived.

The tree closest to him, a grand old thing that had been alive much longer than he, warned his neighbors of an impending storm he could feel in the rarefied air of his uppermost leaves. Those around him agreed then passed the information along to *their* neighbors, the caution spreading through the surrounding wood as far as Artem could hear. Then the conversation turned to other things, mundane subjects that, in a different context, were probably taking place right now on the streets of Portfade.

And his father was going to destroy it all. This was bigger than he'd ever imaged, more important even than Lissa.

No, not more important. This was just another piece of her he hadn't yet seen. He turned.

She stood behind him, surrounded by the chatter of life. There was a change in the conversation as she came closer to the edge of the wood, a *fondness* as they recognized her. It was incredible.

"You don't need to say anything—your face says it all." She laughed, and the Wildwood laughed with her, delighted at her amusement and their part in it.

She led him back to the house, and he blindly put one foot in front of the other, his mind still marveling at what'd he heard.

Back in the house, Lissa's face turned serious. "Now you understand why we have to protect the Wildwood."

"I do. And anything I can do to help, you've got it."

"Given your father's…connections, do you think you can put us in contact with anyone important? Someone who would recognize their sentience and be able to do something about it?" Lissa's face made it painfully clear that all their hopes were riding on him.

"But doesn't Nova have connections to the government? Surely something like this is something they'd want to know—"

Nova shook her head. "It would take too long. Anything I put forward has to go through official channels. And because our…arrangement here isn't well-known…suffice it to say, we'd be jumping through hoops for the next few years. We need someone with an open mind and enough clout to take action *now*."

"So you'd tell this person that the Wildwood is not only alive, but sentient, and that we can talk to it, more or less…and then what?"

"We thought we could get the soldiers to stop burning it, for one."

"Just like that?" Surely they understood that the soldiers were the only thing standing between the

Wildwood and its invasion of the rest of Foxwept? They weren't going to stand aside and let it spread just because it was sentient.

"It's a living thing, Artem. With *consciousness*. What more do they need?" Swift's composure was slipping. He obviously didn't understand how the world worked beyond the Perimeter.

How could he say this delicately? "Swift, I understand how you feel, but— But announcing the fact that the Wildwood is sentient isn't going to be enough. In fact, it's going to make the situation with the rest of the province worse."

"Worse?"

"Well, yeah. Think about it. If they believe us and accept that the Wildwood is a sentient being, they'll hold it responsible for the destruction it's causing."

"But right now they're burning it *alive*." Swift stared at Artem as though he couldn't believe it wasn't that black and white.

"Because it's trying to take over Foxwept. Before the disaster, people lived here, Swift. It was massive agricultural land that fed a large part of the Blackmoth Republic. The Wildwood destroyed all that. And it doesn't seem to be stopping."

"It's trying to survive." Swift stood and pushed himself away from the table. His hands were clenched at his sides.

Lissa stood too. "You guys, we need to—"

Artem held up a hand. "I'm not trying to upset you, Swift. I'm just telling you how they'll think. Believe me, if there's one thing I know something about, it's people not being swayed by emotional appeals."

"So what are you suggesting?"

Remember what the synadroids went through to

prove their sentience. They needed proof of cause and effect, a specific conversation that showed the communication could go two ways, not just plants rambling about wet rot.

"First we need hard evidence to prove it. Can you provide that? Is there some way we could talk to it and it could talk back?" If not then, amazing as it was, their plan had an incredibly slim chance of succeeding.

"That's what we've been working on. Swift's spent the last couple of years trying to learn their language, to communicate with them."

That was exactly the kind of proof they needed. But *trying* wouldn't be good enough. They needed results. "And?"

"And it's a lot harder than I thought," Swift admitted. "It's so nuanced, and there are so many different species...various dialects." He frowned. "Plus, they all talk *a lot*. And quickly. It's difficult for me to keep up. But—" He smiled at Artem's obvious anticipation. "I can communicate with them on a rudimentary level."

"What *exactly* does that mean?"

"I can understand what they're saying, and I can talk back."

There. That was the answer he was hoping for. If Swift could converse with the Wildwood in a practical way, surely that would be all the evidence they needed. "Could you get them to do what you wanted?"

"I can't order them about, if that's what you mean."

That was exactly what Artem had meant. "Not even if you explain to them what's at stake? It probably wouldn't have to be anything huge. Just something, *anything* to demonstrate the possibility of a two-way conversation." The Wildwood didn't have to speak a human language to satisfy the conditions of sentience. It just had to show an ability to understand, and to communicate.

"I don't feel comfortable demanding that they—"

Artem didn't have time for Swift's ideals. "It doesn't matter how *you* feel."

How could he make them understand?

"Look, if whoever we get down here believes that the Wildwood is not only sentient but willing to listen, to cooperate and come to some kind of compromise...that's what we need to happen if there's to be a chance of saving it."

"Would they believe it was real?"

"I don't know. That depends on what happens on the day. I think getting the Wood to *do* something, something that acknowledges its understanding would be our best bet. But..."

"What?"

"Do you think the Wildwood *is* willing to listen? To compromise?"

Swift glanced at Lissa and Nova then shrugged. "All we can do is ask. I'll do what I can—both in terms of proof and the Wood's willingness to deal."

That would have to be good enough for now. He turned to Lissa. "What do you think?"

She sucked on her bottom lip. "I think we're out of options. Mom and Swift will do everything they can to show that the Wildwood can't be destroyed. I trust them. Now we just need someone important enough for us to tell."

"I think I know just the person. An associate of my father."

"A friend of your father? I'm not sure—"

"Associate, not friend. I'm willing to bet he would be more than happy to help bring my father down. And he's got the kind of clout we need. I'll have to use the comms here—I know someone who'll be able to get me right through to him." He ran a hand through his hair; he was not looking forward to this next part. "He should be here by the time I get back."

"Back? Where are you going?"

He faltered. "I'm going to tell my father."

His announcement was *not* taken well.

"Are you *serious*?" The way Lissa was looking at him, the incredulity in her expression made him immediately question himself. "Why in the world would you tell him?"

"Because maybe…maybe he'll figure it's too much hassle and he'll change his mind. He'll abandon anything to do with the Wildwood."

"Do you actually believe that? Or are you just giving him one last chance to be a father and semi-decent human being?"

"That'll never happen. But if I record our conversation, I'll have proof that he knows the Wildwood is sentient. He'll have little choice but to give up." It sounded incredibly naïve, even to his own ears. But at worst, maybe it would buy them more time while his father pondered his next move. He might be willing to risk the law's ire to spy on his son, but knowingly destroying or even exploiting a sentient being as significant as the Wildwood? Not even his father would have the stones for that.

They had a plan. And yet Artem was reluctant to go, to leave things between him and Lissa as they were. They might be able to save the Wildwood, but what about them?

There'll be time for all that. Prove to her first that you're on her side—in every way. And that began with confronting his father.

And if he doesn't budge? What then?

Then we'll keep coming up with plans until he does.

TWENTY-ONE

How many times had he stood outside this door with a heaviness in the pit of his stomach? How many minutes spent waiting for his father to deign to call him in?

Too many.

With any luck, though, this would be the last time. He fingered the recording device in his pocket. *Please let this work*. He'd had to beg his friend Blue for the special contraption. His father was paranoid at the best of times, so there was no way Artem could've slipped a normal recording device past his sweepers. The piece of kit in his pocket was something that Blue had warned him could land him prison for life if he was caught with it, but he hadn't thought twice about the risk. They needed some kind of insurance, and time was short.

The doorman must've seen something in his face, because he simply raised his hands and stepped away from the door.

Artem burst into the office, intending to say his piece before Father could do as much as open his mouth. But it was Artem who was silenced, greeted by the sight of his brother and sister sitting across from their father in what was clearly a family meeting. Now that Artem had defected, was his father going to include them in his plans after all?

Father looked up as he came through the door, his eyebrows raised in mild astonishment. Misha and Luka both glanced over their shoulders but didn't turn.

A whole life with those two, and one word from Father and I'm a ghost.

The only wonder here was that Artem was even a little bit surprised.

"What were you saying, Luka?"

So he was going to just pretend Artem wasn't there? No chance. "I need to speak to you. It's urgent."

Father closed his eyes for a moment, as though waiting for a twinge of pain to pass. "Can you not see we're busy? With family business. The one you're no longer a part of."

"I don't care about that." Not the best way to get his father to listen, but Artem was past diplomacy at this point. "I need to speak to you about the Wildwood."

"Our newest acquisition?"

Artem couldn't disguise his shock. "The deal's already gone through?"

His father laughed and smacked his leg. "Your face."

"Well, has it?"

"As good as. There's still some paperwork and a few checks to be made, but it won't be long. So if you've come to beg me to stop on behalf of your freak girlfriend, you're too late."

He'd wanted to tell Father the truth about the Wildwood in private. But if the deal was already so close to going through, his father would be even more dangerous now, like a wounded animal backed into a corner. Maybe having witnesses wouldn't be a bad thing.

"The Wildwood is a sentient being."

There was barely a moment of silence before Father began laughing again. After a few seconds, his brother and sister joined in.

But he could wait. Let them have their laugh now. He would've done the same a few weeks ago. Besides, the storm that was going to follow when his father realized he was serious would be a typhoon. Best use this time to brace himself.

As Artem stood, unmoving and unreacting, his father's laughter died a slow death. It took Luka and Misha a few seconds to catch on, but eventually their mirth trailed off as well, and the trio regarded Artem with something akin to wariness.

"You can't be serious."

"I am."

"How can you believe that? Is that what your girlfriend told you? And you're so desperate to be with her that you'll believe anything she says?" He addressed Luka and Misha. "She's half-frog, did you know that?"

Artem's hands clenched into fists at his sides. *He's just trying to goad you. Remember why you're here.*

"It's true. The Wildwood is conscious." He held his breath.

"It's not. And even if it was, no one would ever believe it. Since I assume you're going to be making a grand announcement about this, do me a favor and change your last name. I don't want anybody associating our family name with something as ridiculous as this."

Artem couldn't help himself. "You mean our *good* family name? Do you really think I could tarnish it more than you already have?" It was a dangerous path, poking his father's one tender spot. Despite his father's power, he was still a corrupt, immoral ass and everyone knew it. He'd never be accepted by the legitimate powerhouses of Foxwept, although they were more than happy to sit at his table with him. Just not anywhere the public could see.

Father stood, but Artem held his ground. For the first time in his life, there was something human in his father's dead, shark-black eyes. "Why are you here?"

"I want you to leave the Wildwood alone. Yes, because of Lissa, but also because it's the right thing to do. You can't exploit the Wildwood or destroy it knowing it has a consciousness." But even as the words left his mouth, he knew how stupid they were. Of course his father wouldn't care about that—he treated human beings no better. But that wasn't why Artem was here. The device was a comforting weight in his pocket. He just hoped it was doing its job.

"Can't I?" His father laughed again, but there was no humor in it. "Even if you did tell anyone about this ridiculous theory, you have no proof."

"But I do."

His father stared at him for a long moment. "Who else knows about this?"

"No one. I was attempting to talk some reason into you first."

He could practically see the gears in his father's head turning, figuring out his next move. "You will mention this to no one."

"That's not going to happen. We're—"

"Keep this to yourself, and you can still be the boss of Paragon."

His father just didn't get it, did he? The narcissist in him couldn't comprehend that Artem didn't want the title, didn't want anything to do with his father or this wretched family anymore. Even if things didn't work out between him and Lissa, he was done here. Forever.

Luka clearly didn't get it either. He leaped to his feet, overturning his chair as he advanced on Artem. "You can't do that."

Artem sighed. As usual, his brother didn't know his ass from his elbow. "Why are you shouting at *me*, Luka? I don't want the confounded title. Take it with my blessing. *He's* the one you should be shouting at. You're disposable to him."

"I'm not joking, Artem. Do you have any idea how much money is at stake? You will tell no one about this. Even a whisper of this would stop the sale—as you well know." His father cocked his head to the side, as though suddenly seeing a shrewd side of his son he'd never credited him with. "How much?"

It was a fair question. A few weeks ago, he would've named his price, taken the money, and gone on his merry way. But no amount of money was going to get him to back down on this. "I don't want your money."

"What if the sale goes through, but I allow you to manage the Wildwood? That way, you would have the final say in your precious fr—girlfriend's home."

"No deal. You and I both know that's a hollow offer. We're going ahead with this regardless of what you say." He cocked his head, imitating his father's serious look. "It's not always about you, you know."

Father's frown smoothed out into an imperceptible mask. Before this moment, Artem had thought he'd known fear. But now, his father's composure promised that he'd only ever scratched the surface. He was too calm, too still. "So that's your final decision, is it?"

Artem wouldn't let the dread stop him. "Yes. I told you because I was hoping you would let it go, do the decent thing for once." He gave a bitter laugh. "Good thing I'm used to being disappointed by you."

Father pulled on each of his cuffs, snapping them to exactly the right length as he walked back around his desk, shoving Luka hard on the shoulder. "Sit down." He took his chair and folded his hands together on the gleaming surface of his desk. "Anything else you wish to discuss?"

No way. He had to get out of there, now. He'd spent enough time watching his father, unnoticed, to understand, perhaps for the very first time in his life, where they truly stood—nowhere.

"No. I'm going to bed." It took every ounce of courage to turn his back on his father. It was something you should never do with a wild animal, and his father was as feral as they came.

The walk to the door felt longer than it ever had. Every moment he expected something—a bullet, perhaps, or one of those throwing knives Father was so fond of—to stop him from betraying the family he no longer wanted any part of. For even as he escaped unscathed and closed the door behind him, he knew the truth beyond a shadow of a doubt: his father would not let the Wildwood go.

TWENTY-TWO

He almost made it to the front door.

Alexi stepped out of the shadows, his feet silent as a wraith on the marbled floor. "Going somewhere?" He wore a sneer, his scars puckering like a second mouth. One arm hung casually by his side, the other was behind his back, out of sight. He'd always assumed Alexi hated him, watching him from dark corners, skulking about wherever Artem happened to be.

But right now, he didn't have time for the old man's hatred. And to be honest, he was a little insulted. *Alexi* as his executioner? He hadn't expected Father to get his hands dirty, but Alexi? It was too obvious. He'd have preferred someone more poetic, like Luka. Something with a bit of meaning at least.

"I'm leaving, Alexi. For good."

"Back to that frog-girl, eh?"

"She's—" No. No, *that's what she is. And at least he doesn't know her name.* "Yes. Back to my frog-girl. And the minute I see her, I am going to kiss the tips of every single one of her fingers, and then the beautiful webbing between them."

The war raging across Alexi's face was something to behold. *I hope Father has a security camera*

194

watching all this. Truly, the man had missed his calling on the stage. But as amusing as it was to see the hardman so discomposed, his face wasn't important. His left hand was. So far, it stayed where it was. What was he waiting for?

"So you would do that? Turn your back on your family? On your father? After all he's given you?" He rolled his left shoulder. "For some mutant girl you just met?"

You just need to make it through the door. And yet, it wasn't in him to deny Lissa, to diminish her. He willed himself calm, his voice slow and deliberate. "Yes. I would. And not just my father. All of them. All of *this.*" He gestured around him. "I *love* her."

And he was damned if this man was going to stand in their way for one second longer.

There was a flash of metal at Alexi's side as he shifted whatever he was holding in his hand. "I loved your mother, once."

Artem stared at Alexi. He could've sworn the man had just said he'd loved Artem's mother. A crack in his chest that had been long-sealed split open, a wound he'd tried so hard to forget.

His mother. She'd died years ago, an accident, or an illness, depending on who was comforting a grieving child, and as he got older, it was whispers, innuendo, something as dark and secret as the Wildwood and every bit as dangerous. Never spoken about in polite company, or any company at all, if you knew what was good for you.

I loved her.

And that's how I know about Lissa. I've loved before. It was a different kind of love, a deep yearning of the soul rather than an exuberant, unconditional outpouring, but he recognized its face, even after so long.

Alexi wasn't looking at him now, but past him, caught up in the memory. "Before your father, though not by much."

"I— What happened? If you don't mind me asking."

Alexi sucked his lip over his teeth. "Different places, I suppose."

"Places?"

"Classes. I was from the Wildwood, you know. Before it became wild."

Alexi? From the Wildwood?

"Even back then, when it was civilized, we were different from *them*." He waved his hand around the house. "Not as *refined*. They thought us uncouth and savage. And maybe they were right." He scratched his thumb over the stubble on his jaw. "But your mother had a mutation as well."

A mutation? My mother? This was the first he'd ever heard of it. But then, so many parts of his life were shrouded in secrecy. "She did?"

"Yes. A kind heart. A fatal mutation in these circles."

A kind heart. I remember. "How—"

"He'll be coming for you now." Alexi interrupted his reverie.

It seemed as though his questions about his mother were fated to stay unanswered. But Artem would have to mourn that another time. "Are you going to try to stop me?" His gaze flicked to the arm still behind Alexi's back.

"That depended on your answer to my question."

"And?"

"No, I'm not going to kill you. But I won't be able

to hold them off for long, so if you're going to go, do so now."

After Alexi's mercy, what could Artem do? He was reluctant to leave the man behind. "Do you want to come with me? You could find sanctuary in the Wildwood—"

Alexi grinned, revealing a row of metallic teeth. It was the first genuine smile Artem had ever seen from the man. "No, lad, I have no mind to start over. There'll be time for that after I'm dead."

Which, knowing his father, would be sooner rather than later if he knew Alexi had helped Artem escape. "Well, can I at least shock you with that picana?"

Alexi threw his head back and laughed as he withdrew the small rod from behind his back. "No thanks. If I need to, I can do it myself. I may just turn the voltage all the way up to spite your old man." His expression grew grave. "You'd better go, son. And whatever you do, don't come back."

TWENTY-THREE

"You're going to wear a hole in my floor if you keep pacing like that." Swift's voice was mild, but Lissa knew him too well to believe it.

"Don't pretend to be so calm. You're just as anxious about this as I am."

Even if it's not for the same reasons.

Where was Artem? It shouldn't be taking him this long. He was just going to tell his father then come straight back and let them know, or at the very least, send them a message. She checked her comm for the hundredth time. The blank screen mocked her.

There's probably nothing to worry about.

Maybe the best-case scenario had happened. Maybe he'd gone to his father and told him the truth about the Wildwood, and his father had done the decent thing for once, not only for the Wood, but for his youngest son. They'd be free to continue their research and learning, and then, when they were truly ready, they could introduce the Wildwood to those who could protect it. Maybe right now, even as she paced back and forth, Artem and his father were embracing, celebrating the fact they'd found their way back to each other.

You've lost your mind if you think that's even a remote possibility. There's no way that's going to happen. More likely, the worst has happened. Maybe you should be planning for that *instead. What if he betrays you?*

As much as she hated to admit it, there was the tiniest part of her mind that still clung to this possibility like a parasite, leaching her hope. What if he was still only here on behalf of his father, despite what he'd said? What if he was still using her, using them all? She struggled to picture it but...what if he'd simply gone to his father, told him, and right now the two of them were plotting how they could best use this information to their advantage? Would Swift and her mother—and the entire Wildwood—ever forgive her? Would she forgive herself?

"You're doubting him, aren't you?"

Ugh. She should've waited on her own. Fighting the misgivings in her head was bad enough; talking about them would make it even worse. "No. Yes. I—" *Swift is your best friend. Just be honest.* "Yes. What if this is still just some part of their original plan? What if he's there, right now, with his father, laughing at us, clinking lucéat over how they managed to screw over the woodbillies?"

"Or, what if he's on his way here?" He inclined his head and gazed at her. "Why are you doubting him now?"

"Because I—" *Because I doubt myself.* She sat heavily in a chair next to the small table. "Maybe it's me I doubt, not him."

"You?"

"You know, because of my...." She splayed one of her hands out on the table. "I know what you're going to say, Swift, but I just... How could he ever truly care for me, like this?" As it had since the lagoon, hope warred with reason inside her. At their first meeting, Artem had reacted to her the way people always did, dredging up all the usual feelings—shame, awkwardness, defensiveness, like she needed to apologize for what she was. He'd also lied to her, uncaring of the consequences.

But he'd saved her life, kissed her fingers after the storm, reminded her that she should rejoice in what she was. He'd sworn to fight with her to save the Wildwood at the expense of his own family. He obviously felt some kind of connection to her.

But that didn't translate to love. *Maybe I'm just his way out.*

Swift put his hands on her shoulders. "Do you want my opinion?"

She tried to laugh, but all that came out was a twisted hiccup. "When have you ever asked before telling me what you think about something?"

Swift frowned in mock offense. "I have no idea what you mean." Then he sobered. "Lissa, if Artem's fooled you, he's fooled me too. For what it's worth, I believe he truly cares for you. More than that, Liss, I think, well, if he's not already in love with you, he's on his way."

In love with me.

"So no, I don't think he's going to betray you. And I know you think that's the worst-case scenario here, Lissa, but it isn't."

It wasn't? "What could possibly be worse?"

"That his father knows there's no way Artem will betray you."

"I don't understand. If it's as simple as that, why wouldn't he be here by now?"

"His father might not have let him leave." Swift's voice was soft, padding up her spine with tiny clawed feet.

"You mean, you think he's locked him up?"

"Or worse. Lissa, I don't want—"

Lissa clapped her hands over her ears. It was both futile and childish, but she couldn't let Swift finish that sentence. There was no way she could go there right now, no way she could even consider the possibility.

We have to save him. She shot up from the table, crashing into some low-hanging herbs.

"Hey!" Swift darted over, leaping to catch the dry, shattered leaves as they drifted groundward. "What are you doing?"

"We have to help him, Swift. If his father— If there's any truth in what you just said, we have to—" Swift was right. Artem's betrayal wasn't the worst thing that could happen.

"Do what? Storm his house? Knock politely on the door and ask for them to hand him over? We can't—"

Hedwig's perimeter warning flared into life with an ominous sound.

Someone was coming out of the tunnel, approaching the house. "Artem! It has to be." She rushed for the door, but Swift stepped in her way. "What are you doing?"

"Let's make sure he's alone first, yes?"

She hated to wait even another second before knowing that Artem was okay, but Swift was right. She held her breath and watched him come into the clearing where they'd agreed to meet. Finding Swift's house in the Wildwood at night would be near-impossible with his inexperienced eyes. He peered into the dark, trying to see if they were there.

"I think he's alone." Swift was studying an image on his control panel. Then he stuck his head out of the back window and closed his eyes. There was a slight disturbance in the air, and he pulled his head back in. "I can't see anyone else on my HUD, and the Wildwood can't detect anyone." He opened the door for her. "Go on then."

Light spilled out into the Wildwood as Lissa flew down the stairs to meet Artem, but she pulled up short when she saw his face.

His skin was ashen, his mouth a thin line. Something had shaken him, badly. "Artem? Are you— Is everything okay?"

He shook his head. "No, it's definitely not." He leaned over and grabbed one of her hands. "Lissa, I'm so sorry." He led her back up the steps and nodded in approval as Swift locked the door behind them.

"It didn't go well with your father, I take it?" Swift pulled out a chair for Artem at the table.

Artem sat. "No, it went every way *but* well."

Lissa scooted her chair next to his. "What happened? Are you okay? We were starting to get worried." She glanced up at Swift. "We thought maybe your father—"

"Tried to kill me?"

Even though she knew the kind of man Artem's father was, thinking such a thing brought heat to her face. "I'm sorry, I know he's your father. We were just panicking, I think."

"Well, you have every right to, because you are one hundred percent correct."

She couldn't stop the gasp escaping her lips. His own father? When Swift had put the idea out there, the darkness outside, the massive stakes had made it sound plausible, but she hadn't actually *believed* it. What father would do that to his son? Yes, a lot of money was on the line, but wasn't a child's life supposed to be priceless? She couldn't imagine her mother even contemplating such a thing. If Lissa had been part of his family, would he have killed her simply for her mutation?

"He tried to kill you?"

"He's going to. The paperwork for the Wildwood is only a couple of days away from going through. There's simply too much for him to lose."

"You never should've gone to him." She put her hand over his. "I'm sorry. I didn't mean that as a rebuke, just—"

"No, I agree. It's my fault for expecting him to see reason."

"How did you leave it? I mean, you obviously managed to get out."

"Thanks to Alexi. I'll tell you about *that* later," he said to her raised eyebrows. "It was just as big a surprise to me." He ran a thumb over the back of her hand.

"Well, you're here now. And we can keep you safe—"

"You can't, Lissa." He cleared his throat and his hand was suddenly so heavy on hers. "He's going to come after you too."

Cold air filled Lissa's mouth and slid down into her stomach. "Me?"

"And Swift. Possibly even your mother. Anyone who knows the truth about the Wildwood and can prove it. I mean, he may not kill you all, but he's going to need to keep you quiet until the deal goes through, and he's not the kind of man to do things by halves."

Swift was already at the controls, seemingly undisturbed by the price on his head. "We'll just keep moving. He can't kill us if he can't find us. Blue's making contacts for us as we speak. And I can still keep working on—" He narrowed his eyes at the screen.

"Swift? What is it?"

"Someone else is here. Several someones. But it doesn't matter. I just need a few—"

"Artem!" The voice was strong and clear, ringing through Hedwig's walls.

Artem stood and peered out the window, Lissa at his side.

Artem's father stood in the clearing. He raised his hands in the air and turned in a slow circle. "I'm unarmed. I just want to talk."

"Hurry up, Swift." Artem's father—and whoever else he'd brought with him—shouldn't be able to get into Hedwig, but Lissa wasn't willing to take the chance.

"I am, but—"

Artem put his hand on her arm. "I'm going to go and speak to him."

"Artem, you can't. He'll kill you. There are at least two other men hiding out there."

"The fact that he's come himself, not sent Luka or one of his other henchmen...he could be telling the truth. Maybe he wants to make some kind of deal."

Lissa just stared at him. How could he be so blind? Artem knew better than anyone his father couldn't be reasoned with

He turned to her. "Lissa, I have to. I know how risky it is. He's nuts if he thinks I believe he's unarmed, or that we don't know about the other two."

"Then why go? We can just leave right now, just—" Her voice broke. There wasn't going to be a happy ending for them, was there? If he went out there alone, one way or another, she would lose him.

"Lissa…if there's any chance I can save you, I need to take it. Maybe if I can make a deal—" He moved as if on autopilot. "Swift, please open the door."

"Are you sure? We can go now."

Artem shook his head. "It won't do any good. He knows where we are, he'll find out where we're going. The drones, remember? No matter where we go, he'll find us. Our only chance is if I go and speak to him."

If Artem was determined to do this, then he wasn't going to do it alone. Lissa stuck out her chin. "I'm coming with you."

"Lissa—"

"You can't stop me." It was the truth and he knew it. She avoided the anguish in his eyes. They were going to do this together.

Swift pressed a few more keys on his console. "Let's get this over with, then." He shrugged as Lissa opened her mouth to protest. "You can't stop *me*."

They went down the stairs in single file. As they got closer to Artem's father, he crossed his arms over his chest. Lissa couldn't even begin to understand the expression on his face. It lingered somewhere between arrogance and rage, but was oddly stiff, as though he were wearing the mask of a normal person. Bile seared the back of her throat. There was something wrong with Artem's father, something very wrong.

Artem stopped several meters away. "What are you doing here?"

"Why did you leave? I thought you said you were going to bed. I wanted to talk, so I came looking for you."

"To talk?"

"Of course. What else? Look, I know I was angry when we last spoke. I found the news you delivered very…disturbing."

Artem didn't blink. "I found your reaction to my news very disturbing."

"I'm sure. But we can work this out, Artem. We can find a way to—"

"*Your* way, you mean. Don't stand here and act like you're going to make any kind of compromise. You won't. You won't stop until you've gotten exactly what you want."

A muscle in his father's jaw twitched. "Not true. I'm here to make a deal." His voice was so flat, so strangely emotionless. How did Artem ever know if he was telling the truth?

"What kind of deal?"

Why was Artem even asking? There was nothing his father could offer that would be acceptable.

"Artem—" They needed to go back inside now, lock the door and run, never looking back. But the moment for escape had passed. She knew it, and Artem's father knew it too.

"You keep quiet about what you all know until after the deal goes through. Then, as I told you, you and your…girlfriend here can be in charge of how we manage the resources of the Wildwood—"

"I've already said no. We both know damn well how long that arrangement would last." Artem scoffed. "If it even happened in the first place. I have no reason to believe you. You're going to destroy the Wildwood and the lives of the people who live here, just like you destroy everything else."

"And I would never do anything to help you."

Now that Lissa had finally seen Artem's father face to face, he seemed a bit…underwhelming. She'd pictured a man larger than life, fiercer than a cornered bear. But he was as soft as the rest of them, and very, very mortal.

"Ah, so it can speak. Tell me, I mean, I know that men who can swallow their revulsion long enough to bed something of your…ilk must be hard to come by, but doesn't it bother you even a little how he used you? Made you think he could possibly find something as revolting and unnatural as you attractive?" He gave a mock shudder. "It makes my skin crawl just thinking about what he had to do to get the info—"

"Stop." The anguish on Artem's face made Lissa want to fly at his father and claw the smugness off his face with her bare hands. Instead, she stood next to Artem, sliding her hand into his and holding her breath.

He squeezed her hand back, holding it so firmly it hurt, yet she'd never welcomed pain as much. He was here for *her*.

His back was straight, his gaze laser-focused on his father. "There's not going to be a deal. But honestly, you never had any intention of honoring it anyway, did you?"

His father scowled "If you'd stayed when I told you, if you hadn't run off like a coward, yes, I would've at least…considered it. But, because you chose to put your perverse desires over family, well…" He grinned and raised his hands. "There's nothing I can do. When these things are set in motion, they can't be stopped." His grin shattered. "Even if you *beg*."

There was a flash of light then everything moved

quickly, too quickly, and the next thing Lissa knew, Artem and Swift were both held fast, their arms pinned behind their backs, by two of Andrei's henchmen, and Lissa found herself with her back to Andrei's chest, a small rod of metal pressed to her throat. The burst of light still burned in her retinas, and her brain scrambled to keep up.

"Don't move, any of you, or I'll give the frog a shock that will stop her heart."

She kept her voice as steady as her body. "Let go of me."

"I'd listen to her if I were you." Swift was calm, taking in the entire scene with only mild interest. Only Artem struggled, his face flushed as he fought to free himself from a man he'd known his entire life.

Andrei laughed, a sound that made Lissa's jaw ache to snap together until her teeth splintered. "And why would I do that? I'm not a fly—what's she going to do?" His laugh caught in his throat as he staggered a bit. "Now that you see how things are, Artem, perhaps you'll realize just how foo—how foolish you've been."

He glanced down at his fingers holding the shock device to Lissa's throat. "My fin... Numb. I don't... Why is your sk-skin like stars?" His arm dropped a little, and his legs began to buckle.

It was true. All over Lissa's body, her skin gleamed. She'd once been terrified of it, a symbol of her curse. But not today. Today she'd never been more grateful for what she was.

The man holding Artem gave him a rough shake. "What's happening?"

Artem stared at her. "I don't know. Lissa?"

Lissa's voice carried across the clearing, steady and strong. "Have you ever wondered how certain frogs defend themselves? No fangs, no claws. No powerful friends to hide behind?"

Artem's father didn't answer. He slumped to his knees, his arms still wrapped around Lissa. She twisted around. She was reflected in his eyes, a pale-faced, fire-haired girl whose divergence was the start of an era he would never see.

"We've had to evolve other ways to fight, to defend ourselves." She sank to her knees as well and gently maneuvered Artem's father into her arms like an oversized child. "The poison will paralyze your entire body, and eventually, you'll stop breathing."

"St—stop it, and I'll leave the...leave..." His shoulder twitched as though he was trying to raise his arm, make one last deal to save himself.

Lissa shook her head. "There's nothing I can do. When these things are set in motion, they can't be stopped." She smiled sadly. "*Even* if you beg."

Silence descended as the Wildwood itself held its breath, waiting for Andrei Volkov to take his last. There was no gasp, no rattle, no ferocious death-cry. The next breath simply didn't come.

The man holding Artem shoved him to the ground. "Is he dead?" He sprinted over to where Andrei lay in Lissa's lap, his mouth slack and eyes still focused on her face, the vision he'd carried with him into the dark. "You *killed* him?"

Lissa raised her head. "Would you blame the frog for poisoning you? Or would you blame yourself for laying your hands on it?"

The man bared his teeth at her. "Well, I don't need to touch you, so—" He struggled as Artem trapped his arms behind him. "I'll—"

Swift spoke softly into the night, a litany no human could hear. The Wildwood seemed to give a throaty laugh, the voluptuous joy of a woman about to have her heart's delight. A pair of thick vines snaked across the ground, their barbed tips gleaming in the moonlight. The man holding Swift let go and tried to sprint away, but the creepers were too quick. They coiled around the men's legs, their spines biting deep into the flesh as they twined up their bodies and held them fast. Both men tried to scream, but their cries cut off as the twisting plants slithered down their throats. Their prey secured, the vines retracted into the shadows, dragging the men with them. Even the whites of their eyes soon disappeared, and finally, they were alone.

Swift closed his mouth.

"Lissa." Artem began to sprint toward her but stumbled when he was only halfway, his left leg suddenly unable to bear his weight. He fell to his knees, his expression confused. He crawled toward her, dragging his leg.

"Artem?" Had the man holding him hurt him? She tried to push his father's dead weight off her, but he remained as obstinate in death as he'd been in life. "Swift, what's wrong with him? Help him!"

Swift bent over him, running his hands over the length of his body. "Artem? Where does it hurt?"

"My leg." He let out a string of curses as Swift rolled up the hem of his pants. A long, angry-looked scarlet line ran up the side of his calf. Already the skin around it was beginning to redden and swell.

Swift glanced up at Lissa. "The blightvine must've caught him on its way past." He gave Artem a pained grin. "I think that's going to leave a scar."

Artem grinned weakly back. "But that's a good thing, right? You only get scars if you survive." When Swift didn't answer, the smile fell from his face. "I *am* going to survive, aren't I?"

"Swift?" Why wasn't he answering Artem? He spent most of his spare time cataloging the plants and, for the dangerous ones, their antidotes, so why did he look so uneasy?

"Of course," he mumbled. "I just have to fetch the antidote. I'll be right back."

As he dashed away, Lissa gave another mighty shove, this time managing to heave Andrei off her. He landed face-down and for a minute she held her breath, not entirely convinced he was dead. When he didn't move, she crawled the few feet between her and Artem and pulled as much of him onto her lap as would fit.

She stroked his forehead. The skin there was damp and burned with unnatural heat. *Hurry up, Swift.* "Is the pain bad?"

He managed a small smile. "No. I mean, it's not pain, exactly, more of a numbness...like parts of me are flying away, while others are sinking into the ground." He blinked up at her. "I'm still all here though, aren't I?

She smiled. "Yes, you are. Artem, I'm so sorry about this. And about your father."

Artem dismissed his father with a feeble wave. "It's okay, Lissa. He would've killed you, one way or another. He's gotten away with so much over the years he'd forgotten just how mortal he was." He twisted his head to look over where his father lay. "Besides, he died doing what he loved—being a complete bastard."

"Well, I'm still sorry. Artem, I—"

"I love you, Lissa."

"Artem—"

"I mean it. I *love* you. I think it started that day

at the lagoon. It took me by surprise. I mean, we barely knew each other and—"

"And I'm a frog-girl." There was no pain as she said it; there never would be again.

"But that's just it. I didn't fall in love with you despite it. I fell in love with you *because* of it. All my life, I wanted to leave Foxwept. I never felt like I really belonged here, in the life that I had. But when I met you, I began to realize I didn't need the rest of the world to find it. It was here, rarer and more wonderful than I could've ever dreamed it to be." He tried to raise his hand to her cheek, and as it failed, she lifted it for him and pressed it to her lips.

"I love you too. I belong here, but I've always felt that something was missing. I thought I was going to have to leave the Wildwood, travel the Blackmoth Republic to find it, but I think that piece was you."

She would've searched every inch of the Republic to find what she felt for Artem. But instead of falling in love with him, she was soaring toward it, her arms wide. They'd journeyed further than they'd realized, had managed to close the impossibly wide distance between them. Perhaps when everything was done with the Wildwood, they'd make a new journey, the one they'd always dreamed of separately. Only now they would do it together, searching for nothing.

She dipped her head and kissed him. "I love you," she whispered into his lips. They curled into a smile as he whispered it back and—

His eyes widened as his back arched. His hand was ripped away from her face while his body twisted, wrung by invisible hands, before slamming against the earth again. He was having some kind of seizure. And where the hell was— "Swift! *Hurry.*" No. Not now. It had been only a scratch, the tiniest mark. "Swift!"

Artem's eyes rolled back in his head and he clawed at the ground, uprooting the Wildwood as he fought to stay alive. She wrapped her arms around him and held him as tightly as she could, pressing his head to her chest and rocking him back and forth as though she could soothe the venom from his veins.

"Swift." It was a plea, a prayer.

"I'm here." He was next to her, pressing a diffuser to Artem's neck.

"It's too late. He's dead, Swift. He—

Artem opened his eyes, moon-pale and luminous as a pearl. They searched immediately for Lissa's face, and the moment they found her, he smiled.

"Artem?" She brushed the hair back from his face. Why did his eyes look like that? "Are you okay? You—"

"I...I *think* I'm okay. I feel... I *feel*. I can feel everything now. Everything is clearer. I can see... Can you hear them, Lissa?"

He was alive, and she was grateful for that, but what was wrong with him? Was he hallucinating? "Swift, what's happening to him?"

Swift looked at her, his eyes wide. "I'm so sorry. I didn't make it back in time."

"But you did. He's..." She wouldn't say *fine*, but—

"He's becoming."

"Becoming? Becoming what?"

"Of the Wildwood."

EPILOGUE

Why was she so nervous? They'd practiced this a dozen times—it was going to work. *It has to*. At least the weather was good, the sun shining its blessing down over the clearing at the edge of Wildholde.

She wasn't the only one holding her breath. Artem stood next to her, his hand gripping hers so hard she'd already elbowed him in the ribs. Twice.

"Artem! You're squeezing again."

"Sorry." His grip loosened—momentarily.

She didn't really mind. He could squeeze her hand like a vise forever if it meant they were together.

His eyes had eventually returned to their normal color, but whenever they used him to produce an antidote, they would again become milky and opaque as though he went to another place entirely.

As she'd cradled Artem in the Wildwood, Swift had explained what he thought had happened.

"Swift, stop speaking in riddles. What do you mean he's becoming of the Wildwood?"

"You had a dormant mutation that was triggered by your exposure to the same elements as the Wildwood, right? I think Artem is the same. When the blightvine wounded him, its venom triggered some dormant mutation inside him."

A mutation? Like hers? "What kind of

mutation?"

"I think he's immune to its venom."

It turned out that Artem's mutation made him immune not only to the venomous barbs of the blightvine, but to most of the poisonous plants and animals in the Wildwood. Even more incredible, they found he was also able to synthesize antidotes for them. A venom could be injected into Artem's veins, and only a short time later, the blood drawn from him would contain the antibodies needed to neutralize the venom. Yet another phenomenon of the Wildwood.

And if they were lucky, today they would be able to prove its greatest miracle.

So much was riding on this demonstration of the Wildwood's sentience. The governor had given them four months to prepare their proof. And he'd insisted that the proof not only be obvious to the scientific community but also to the laymen of Foxwept, a demonstration that everyone could understand. If they were successful, Lissa's mother would officially take the helm, with Swift as her right-hand man and official linguist and liaison.

And then…Foxwept would gain yet another jewel in its crown. The plans being discussed for its future were tentative but immense. Foxwept Governor Suluk, who'd advocated for the emancipation of the synadroids two years prior, had agreed that if the Wildwood could, in fact, be proven to be sentient, he would petition the Blackmoth Republic for it to officially be allotted the massive swath of land it occupied. In return, the Wildwood would have to agree that it would no longer spread or encroach on any other part of Foxwept Province or the Blackmoth Republic.

Governor Suluk even hoped that one day a system of trade could be established between the Wildwood and the rest of Foxwept Province. His mind spun with the same possibilities as Andrei's had, only he planned to use them for the benefit of all, not for profit. In fact, he intended to make profiting off the Wildwood illegal for anyone who wasn't already a member of the newly designated region. And even those who had the rights to it would be carefully monitored to ensure that the wellbeing of the Wildwood was paramount.

"If only my father were here to see this." Artem's smile was wistful. "It would kill him all over again."

"Artem, shush." Andrei's death had not been mourned, nor particularly investigated. Perhaps if his body had been found there would've been a basis for investigation, but as no trace of him or his henchmen was ever recovered, his death was classified as a mysterious misadventure and signed off on without ceremony.

Artem had relinquished any claim to his father's estate or the business to his brother Luka. Now that his father was dead, his sister had decided she *did* want to run the business, but he would let the two of them fight it out. He and Lissa hadn't been back to the house since he'd left it that night. He'd shed it like an old skin and been reborn.

In fact, once this demonstration was over, if it were a success, both Lissa and Artem would be free. Lissa glanced at her comm. They still had plenty of time.

"Why is this taking so long?" She hadn't been to many—well, any—events like this before, but people had been milling around now for nearly an hour. Everyone was here, so what was the delay?

"The governor likes a bit of pomp and ceremony." Artem laughed. "I remember one time, he—"

Governor Suluk's voice boomed out over the crowd of people from Wildholde and the large group he'd handpicked to bear witness. "People of Foxwept, and especially those of the Wildwood, I would like to welcome you all to what we hope will be a new era for our beloved province. You all know why we're here today, and I know how eager you are for us to start."

Eager? More like anxious, worried, terrified...there was so much riding on today. Anything could go wrong.

"Let us begin." He turned to Swift, who stood at the edge of the clearing in front of a large oak tree and put a friendly hand on his shoulder. "Show us what you've got."

Swift addressed the crowd without preamble. "We're here today to prove that the Wildwood is sentient. Sentient in such a way that its members can think, communicate with each other, suffer. That it *feels* emotions—like those you and I feel."

Lissa was impressed; Swift was a natural at this. If it had been her in front of the crowd, she would've probably just kept saying the same sentence over and over.

"Years ago, we discovered that the Wildwood communicated through ultrasonics. Its inhabitants spoke to each other. Their conversations were nothing extraordinary, just simple exchanges you've likely had with your own neighbors a hundred times. Eventually, we managed to decode that language, to approximate it to our own. As a result, we've been able to create translation software that will convert our languages for each other. Now, this program is still not perfect, there's much work to be—"

Lissa shook her head and waved at him. *Stop. It's time.*

"Please press the button on each of your earbuds and insert them in your ears."

At first, the crowd hesitated. Then, following the enthusiastic example of Governor Suluk, they obeyed. Would they be able to hear what they couldn't before, a symphony of life all around them? Would the Wildwood cooperate, allow themselves to be heard en masse, revealing itself to the very people who'd worked so hard to destroy it?

There was a collective intake of breath then a multitude of emotions rippled through the crowd. Whispers of fear at first, then wonder.

Lissa slipped her own earbuds in.

They filled with voices, layered on top of each other.

"They are looking at us, can you tell? Can they hear us?—"

"Do they know about the storm in two days? They must know—"

"The wither beetles are on the move again. Be careful, they always start at the root—"

"If you want to get rid of them, you need to—"

She went over to Swift and squeezed his shoulder. "I think you've done it." She nodded toward Governor Suluk. A single tear ran from under his closed lids as he listed to the symphony of mundane chatter around him. There was no mystery here, no haunting. The Wildwood was magic, true, but it was the fairy tale of life, of the existence of millions of beings born from a disaster to rise as a phoenix.

Suluk opened his eyes. "So it's true."

Swift smiled gently. "Yes. We...we would've brought this to you earlier, but we wanted to be sure we could prove it to you. We hoped that if we could, you'd put a stop to the destruction of the Wood at the Perimeter. And veto any plans to destroy it or harm it in any way in the future."

Governor Suluk nodded, but his expression turned grave. "It *is* a miracle, I'm sure we can all agree on that, but—"

"But?"

"But I'm afraid it's not enough. Simply being sentient isn't sufficient for us to lay down our arms against it." He held up his hand as Swift began to protest. "You have to understand, the Wildwood threatens the rest of the Foxwept Province and has done so for the last eight years. Just because it has a consciousness doesn't mean it can run wild. It can't have it both ways. If the Wildwood wants to be treated like the sentient and legal citizens of Foxwept Province, it needs to show the same respect and adherence to our laws. At the moment, its continuing encroachment violates those laws."

Artem warned us about this. Lissa had hoped that the miracle of the Wood's consciousness would be enough proof, that the finer details could be discussed later, but that clearly wasn't the case. Now what? They'd come too far for this to be the end.

Maybe if we can have just a bit more time, we could come up with a plan, could find something to—

But it seemed Swift wasn't done. "I understand, Governor Suluk." He handed the governor a comm he'd finished designing only the week before. It allowed the holder to speak to the Wildwood, but what difference would that make? The Wildwood already knew it was at war with Foxwept. Swift then passed him another comm. "This second one here is in contact with the Perimeter."

The governor looked as confused as Lissa felt. Tentatively, he spoke into the comm. "Hello?"

The voice on the other end was as clear as though the woman speaking stood next to them. "Governor Suluk? This is Lieutenant-Colonel Pont. We're ready, sir."

Lissa darted to Swift's side. Whatever he was up to, he hadn't included her in the plan. "What's going on?"

Swift gave her one of his enigmatic smiles. "Just watch." But there was an anxiety lurking under his grin that tightened Lissa's own throat.

The governor looked questioningly at Swift. "Mind telling me what you've got planned?"

"Speak into that comm there." He pointed to the first device he'd handed the governor. "Introduce yourself to the Wildwood. Tell it what it will take for you to accept its sentience and membership as a citizen of Foxwept."

"I—" Suluk turned to Lissa's mother. "Is he serious?"

Nova nodded. "You said you needed more from it."

Governor Suluk lifted the comm to his mouth and spoke. "Uh, members of the Wildwood, I am Mark Suluk, Governor of Foxwept Province. I understand you've been told why I'm here today. First, I would like to acknowledge your sentience."

There were murmurs in the crowd and Lissa strained to decipher their meaning. Some seemed confused, other wary, but most were simply as curious as she was.

"I know the last eight years have been difficult—for all of us. Until now, the inability for us to communicate has resulted in a number of casualties on both sides.

Mostly on our side. But she caught herself. This day was about healing their wounds, not opening them further.

"However, today we are able to open a line of communication between us. I would like to use this opportunity to extend a welcome to the newest members of our province."

A rustle rippled through the Wildwood and the crowd drew closer together, their whispers hushed as the governor continued.

"However, in order for this offer to succeed, we will need you, the Wildwood, to abide by the current laws of our Province, and those we will put in place to honor and protect your sentience and recognition as citizens.

"In order for us to proceed, I will need assurances from you that you will no longer encroach outside the boundaries we've set for you. Your existence is not your fault, and your proliferation across our land was not malicious. We are willing to grant you the land you already occupy as long as you cooperate with regards to reasonable access for those who occupied these lands before you."

He paused and assumed a more formal posture. "Therefore, please, give us some sign of your agreement, some act of good faith that we can use as a foundation going forward."

There was silence from the crowd, from Governor Suluk, and from the Wildwood itself as they all seemed to hold their breaths.

What would happen? How would the Wildwood

respond? Would it be able to forgive? Would it accept these conditions? Would it trust?

The ground beneath Lissa's feet tremored slightly then stopped. Was that the sign? "Artem? Did you fee—" The tremors began again, stronger this time, and a low hum seemed to emanate from the Wildwood.

Lieutenant-Colonel Pont's voice flew through the comm. "Governor? Are you all right? Is the ground shaking where you are?"

The governor clutched at the comm like a lifeline. "Yes. I assume it's the same at the Perimeter?"

"Yes, sir, do you think it's— Governor! Sir!" Pont's voice distorted then disappeared.

"Pont? Pont!" the governor shouted into the comm.

The comm squealed back to life again. "It's moving sir, the Wildwood. It's—"

The canopy of the Wildwood seemed to dissolve, fragmenting upward as thousands of birds soared into the sky.

"Is it attacking?" He spun to face Swift, his cheeks deeply flushed in his pale face. "Was this some sort of ruse?"

Swift held up both hands. "No! It's not. I don't—"

Lissa rushed to his side. "It's not a trick—" she said, but her voice was lost in the roar of the crowd as they squeezed even tighter together in fear, even those who'd lived in the Wildwood for years.

It was clear just how afraid of the Wildwood they really were. What would happen if the Wildwood *did* become a citizen? When it was exposed to the rest of the province, there would also be a spotlight on it.

And by proxy, on her. Would people be as afraid of her? Had this been a terrible mistake?

Artem squeezed her hand. *No.* This was the way it had to be. They just had to trust that what was happening was part of it.

Governor Suluk was still trying to get a clear response from the Perimeter. "Pont? What's going—"

"It's withdrawing, sir!"

"Withdrawing? What do you mean?" At the sound of his shout, the crowd began to quiet again, straining to hear.

"The plants are moving back from the Perimeter. I—I don't know how they're doing it. It's as though they're walking on stilts, pushing themselves out of the ground. I've never seen anything like it—"

The crowd around Lissa erupted, and she clutched Artem's hand. What would they do, if they became scared enough? Would they turn on those who'd brought them here? On Swift? On her mom? It was another five minutes of Governor Suluk waving his arms for their attention before they quieted enough to hear Pont's voice again through the comm. "...they seem to have settled again, sir. They've pulled back about twenty feet."

"Thank you, Pont. Standby." He raised his voice to placate the throng. "As you've just heard, everything is fine. The Wildwood was simply doing what we requested of them. You have nothing to fear."

Then he addressed the Wildwood. "I assume that your withdrawal from the Perimeter is your assurance that you will abide by the laws of our Province from now on?"

There was a gust of air, a collective sigh. Then a

single reply came through the comm, in millions of voices. "Yes."

"Then I would like to officially welcome you, as the Governor of Foxwept, to our Province. It's been a long time coming, and I know that the transition won't be easy for any of us, given the animosity that's existed for so many years. However, we will work on this together, and I look forward to being present at your citizenship ceremony in the future. In the interim, however, I would like to speak with you about a few issues. Do you, uh, have a governor yourself? I have some important matters to discuss with whoever you hold in that regard."

The governor looked around at the crowd, surprised, as though they'd interrupted an official meeting. "Some privacy, please?" After everyone present had removed their earbuds, he addressed the Wildwood, keeping his voice low, his words unintelligible. He spoke at length, laughing softly and nodding. The Wildwood responded in kind, seeming to vibrate with mirth, to sway and move in a pattern too coincidental to be random.

The crowd, still unable to fully comprehend everything that had just happened, milled around the clearing, until those from Wildholde appeared with refreshments, and proposed a toast that was accepted with great relish.

It's going to take a while for people to accept what's happened here today, and I'm sure not all of them will. But that was a problem for another day.

After a time, Artem clapped the governor on the back, and he reluctantly pulled out one of his earbuds.

"Well? What do you think?"

The governor shook his head slowly. "I think the

population of Foxwept just got a whole lot bigger." He turned to Nova and Swift and grinned. "Whatever you need, you've got it. From this moment, the Wildwood is under the full protection of Foxwept and the Blackmoth Republic. I will personally see to it." He shook his head once more. "What an incredible world we live in."

He then caught sight of Lissa. He took in her mutation, the parts of her she swore to no longer hide. "Young lady— I believe you're Nova's daughter?"

"Yes." Now what? Was he going to ask her the same intrusive questions people always did?

"Artem—and our mutual friend—has told me about you and your..."

"Mutation." She said it with pride. If the Wildwood could reveal itself to the entire world, so could she.

"Yes, your mutation. May I speak with you about it?"

"Of course." She braced herself. The crowd were still speaking amongst themselves; no one was listening.

"As I am sure you know, you're not the only one who has, since the Wildwood, manifested these...changes."

That was true. "No. I know of a few others here in the Wildwood, though theirs is not as...visible as mine."

He nodded, rubbing his darkly whiskered chin. "And it appears it hasn't just happened in the Wildwood."

That was news to her. Her heart leaped. There were others in the rest of the Province? Others like her?

"In fact, it seems to be happening all over. Not in huge numbers, but enough that I, as governor, would be remiss not to take it into consideration."

Take it into consideration. That sounded ominous. Before, invisibility had been her main saving grace. "Oh? What's causing it? Do you know?"

He sighed. "Not exactly, though we suspect it may be transferred by mosquito bites. Insects that have migrated from the Wildwood to other parts of the Province."

The breath caught in Lissa's throat. *The Wildwood couldn't cause mutations, but if one was already there...* "Not everyone who gets bitten mutates. Am I right?"

He bobbed his head. "Yes, completely. Otherwise, we'd all be changed. It seems that, as in your case, a small percentage of people have a dormant mutation that's triggered and manifests when they're bitten by this type of mosquito. This is all very new information, but we expect to begin work on a vaccine as soon as possible— Only for those who wish to take it, of course," he added hastily.

Had her shocked expression been that obvious? "I still don't understand what that has to do with me. If you think you're going to use me as some poster girl for why people should take the vaccine—"

"No, no, of course not! The opposite, in fact. Well, not quite. Sorry, I'm making this very confusing. It's been that kind of day." He ruffled his hand through the front of his salt-and-pepper hair.

"Governor?" Did he need to sit down? He was very flushed, and a sheen of sweat shone on his forehead.

"I'm just very excited, you see. It's funny, really. My grandmother once spoke of a time when people like you, Lissa, were not uncommon. Not in her time, of course, nor her grandmother's, but still within our family's memory." His gaze softened, looking past them into another time. He shook himself. "Sorry, there I go again. What I wanted to ask you concerns a project I wish to start. It's not going to be easy for these young people—indeed, it seems to be mostly young people who are affected—to adjust to their new physiognomies. As they become more public, there may be pushback from the rest of society for a while, and even their own families might initially reject them—though, of course, we will be doing as much as we can to normalize them."

He straightened proudly. "I would like to build an academy in Foxwept where they can live and go to school, one that will give them the opportunity to feel comfortable until the rest of us have caught up—their choice, of course. No one would be forced to attend." He smiled at her and extended his hand. "And I would like you to help me. And Artem too, of course."

An academy? For mutants like her? It seemed too good to be true. But the governor's face was open and honest, clearly eager for her support.

What could she say? "I— I would love to." The words left her mouth before she could think it through. But it was the right answer.

"Wonderful!" The governor beamed as he shook her hand—her *bare* hand. "I look forward to hammering out the details. I'll be in touch. Now, if you don't mind—" He stuffed the buds back into his ears and turned his attention back to the Wildwood.

"Well, that was a surprise." Artem suppressed a grin.

"You knew!" How had he managed to keep that secret? But it didn't matter. "Can you believe it? An academy, for people like me—like us." What would her life have been like, if she'd been able to grow up among her peers? "I hope the rest of Foxwept is ready for us."

He put his arm over her shoulder. "It won't be, of course, but it's a start."

They walked over to her mother and Swift, and motioned for them to come away beyond the crowd. She wouldn't tell them about Governor Suluk's plan just yet. Today was their day. They followed her to a shady, quiet corner where they could speak freely.

There she threw her arms around both of them. "Congratulations. I think you've convinced them all."

Nova smiled, but the weariness etched into her face made Lissa's heart ache. Convincing Governor Suluk was only the beginning. There was so much to do, so many oncoming storms to weather. But they'd done it. The Wildwood had been saved, and with any luck, would flourish. All both sides had to do was hold up their ends of the bargain. There would likely be problems down the road that none of them could yet anticipate, but those were worries for another day.

Artem slipped his arm around her shoulders and squeezed her gently. "Come on, Lissa, or we're going to be late."

He was right. They'd lingered as long as they could. But still she was reluctant to go. Today had been such an important day for her mother, for Swift—for them all.

Her mother laughed. "Lissa, *go*. Everything will be fine. It's not like you're going away forever or to the other end of the planet. We'll be fine, won't we, Swift?"

He grinned. "Of course we will. Do you want me to take you? Hedwig is just beyond the clearing."

Months ago, in the aftermath of that fateful night, Artem and Lissa had booked a trip around the Blackmoth Republic. They'd planned to spend months traveling, finally discovering the world they'd both been searching for, that had always been just beyond their reach.

But no longer. Only a few more steps and they'd have everything they wanted.

When they were finally close enough, they leaped from Swift's threshold and sprinted the remaining distance.

Artem continued to fret. "We're going to miss it."

Had he always worried this much? "No, we're not." They would be just in time.

They raced up the steps. "If we miss it—"

"Artem, we're not going to miss it!"

And they didn't. As they settled into their seats on the roof terrace of their brand-new cottage alongside the lagoon, the sun sank just beyond the horizon and the sky turned from red to indigo.

Lissa held her breath. *Here it comes.*

The sky erupted into showers of multicolored light, cascading down through the stars as the luminous threads blazed across the sky. It happened only once a year, the herald of new beginnings.

"It's amazing." He turned to her and smiled. "And to think we get to see this all from our own doorstep."

She nestled into him and watched the radiance

twisting and dancing across the sky. All their lives she and Artem had been searching for something missing from their lives, something they'd thought existed only outside themselves.

How wrong they'd been.

They still wanted to travel the Blackmoth and beyond, one day. But for now, it could wait. Each had found what they'd longed for in the other, and in their own hearts, a place which had been as mysterious and impenetrable as the Wildwood itself. But now, like the brilliance of the fire streaking above their heads, and the vibrant whispers of life all around, love had illuminated every shadow inside them, opening an entire world before them, a world that was solely theirs to explore.

ABOUT THE AUTHOR

A.W. Cross is a made of 100% star stuff and writes social science-fiction and futuristic romance. She lives in the wilds of Canada with her beloved family and a deep nostalgia for the 80s.

Other books by A.W. Cross:

FOXWEPT ARRAY

Rose, Awake: A Futuristic Romance Retelling of Sleeping Beauty (Foxwept Array Short Story)

Pine, Alive: A Futuristic Romance Retelling of Pinocchio (Foxwept Array #1)

Clara, Dreaming: A Futuristic Romance Retelling of The Sandman (Foxwept Array #2)

Beauty Unmasked: A Futuristic Romance Retelling of Beauty and The Beast (Foxwept Array #3)

THE ARTILECT WAR

The Seeds of Winter: Artilect War Book One

The Gardener of Man: Artilect War Book Two

The Harvest of Souls: Artilect War Book Three

The Artilect War Complete Series